the BOW of ANARCHY

STARFELL BOOK THREE

JESSICA RENWICK

Published by Starfell Press

Starfell Book Three
The Bow of Anarchy

ISBN (hardcover) 978-1-7753871-9-0
ISBN (paperback) 978-1-7753871-8-3
ISBN (eBook) 978-1-989854-00-6

Cover Page design by Ebook Launch
Edited by Talena Winters
Formatted by Red Umbrella Graphic Designs
Proofread by Erin Dyrland.
Author Photo © Bonny-Lynn Marchment. Used by permission.

Printed in the United States of America, or the country of purchase.

The Starfell series:

The Book of Chaos

The Guitar of Mayhem

The Bow of Anarchy

The Curse of the Warlock (2021)

The Star of Truth (2022)

Other works by Jessica Renwick:

The Haunting of Lavender Raine

The Witch's Staff (part of the Mythical Girls anthology by
Celticfrog Publishing)

Praise for The Book of Chaos

"Author Jessica Renwick has crafted a highly engaging tale about the love of family and the true bonds of friendship. This enchanting tale offers a thrilling adventure for young readers who are sure to be entertained by this first book in the Starfell Series."
– Children's Literary Classics Book Awards & Reviews

"Renwick has designed an imaginative world for her story with rich details without letting description getting in the way of action. Book One of this series is a quick, delightful read that leaves you wondering what those kids will get up to next!"
– Karina Sinclair, editor at Line by Line Studios.

"Renwick weaves a wonderful story filled with twists and turns and exciting new characters that are definitely going to draw in even the most reluctant readers in your household."
– Patrick McNulty, author of the Milo Jenkins: Monster Hunter series.

2019 Children's Literary Classics Gold Award Winner for Middle Grade General

2019 Book Excellence Award Winner for Children's Fiction

2019 Story Monsters Approved

"Feelings are much like waves, we can't stop them from coming, but we can choose which one to surf." – Jonathan Martensson

Please note: I have put together a glossary of unfamiliar words, names, and world-specific terms that is located at the end of the book.

Prologue

Endora jabbed the gnarled wand at the fallen star laying on her desk next to the open leather-bound book. A crimson poof of smoke emanated from the wand's tip and wafted over the glittery rock. It lay there, shimmering in the dim light of her library with no reaction. If anything, the lich could have sworn it gave off a glint of cheeky disobedience.

"Wretched stick!" The lich hurled the wand across the desk. It hit the mahogany bookcase beside it, almost crashing into an empty frame that hung on the wall. A noise like the sound of a car backfiring exploded throughout the library. The shelf splintered and its books toppled to the floor, burying the wand beneath them.

Endora huffed and glanced into the mirror above her desk. Her usually-sleek ebony hair had pulled from its twist, framing her smooth ivory face with fly-away strands. Her amethyst eyes flashed scarlet as she tried to smooth the stray hairs.

She hadn't been sure the magic wand would work. After all, its creator and the source of its power had died over a century ago. But when she'd read about it in the Magic and Lore of Starfell, the giant tome that held all the secrets of this land, she'd sent her henchman, Doug, after it. And he found the wand—buried beneath the heavy soil of Stonebarrow with its creator. Luckily, Doug knew a thing or two about digging up graves.

Endora scowled at the pile of fallen books in front of the bookcase. But it was all for nothing.

"Careful, Ma'—er—Mistress." The man's gravelly voice came from the corner of the room. Endora had been so focused on trying to break the star's curse, she hadn't noticed the brown fog pooling around her ankles that signalled the man's arrival.

He rocked back on his heels, a toothpick between his brown teeth and an amused look on his haggard face. "Yeh don't wan' ter destroy the whole place. Yeh need yer picture frames if yer gonna survive."

"You think I don't know that?" Endora snarled at him. "If I could unlock this star, I wouldn't need those frames. With its power, I'd never age. My magic would be the strongest in all of Starfell." She gritted her teeth and whirled on him. "And you—you're not helpful at all, are you? Perhaps you'd be most useful to me inside one of my frames."

Doug held his hands up and took a step back. "Hey, now, yer underestimating ol' Doug." He pointed at the softly glowing book on her desk. "I still say yeh gotta look in there again. Somethin's missin'."

"Obviously!" White-hot rage rose from Endora's toes to the top of her head. Her strength seeped away from her. Her knees buckled and she caught herself on the edge of the desk.

"Careful, Mistress," Doug chided. "Maybe yeh need a break?"

Endora glowered at him, then righted herself and glanced down at the book. Curled script scribbled frantically across the page.

The aging crone straightens, staring directly into my pages with pent-up frustration. If only she knew how simple the answer is, she'd have the key to everything she wants.

"Argh!" Endora slammed her balled-up fist on the desk, causing the pages to ruffle. The star skittered sideways, away from the book.

Anger and threats will do nothing to unlock the secret. If only she could look into her past and remember what she created so long ago—when she was capable of feeling love and affection.

Endora's throat tightened, memories unfurling inside her. The smiling face of her first born son, who left a trail of blossoming flowers wherever he went, beamed at her. Fierce protectiveness roared within her as she remembered the night the police had come to take him away—merely for having magic. She reached for the boy and a white light ignited in her chest, causing the vision to fade.

The book shuddered and hummed, then leapt from the desktop in a whirl of flapping pages.

Endora jolted, horrified at the warm glow around her.

What's going on? No!

She swatted at the light around her, trying to beat it into submission. Her magic—lich magic—should be red. A pulsing, boiling, raging scarlet that burned the air and struck fear into her enemies' hearts. Her skin writhed at the pure whiteness that now flowed from her.

"Mistress, the book!" Doug shouted.

The book fell back to the desk with a thump. The pages whipped to a spot near the beginning. The Blood Curse glared out at her in blood-red ink.

Endora's eyes widened. She thrust both palms against the table on either side of the book, gazing into its pages with manic desperation.

It was a list of ingredients. They started out simple enough, with components common to most spells.

Yarrow, wormwood, camphor . . . But as the list went on, the components grew more complex with rare items only meant for the most powerful spells.

- A feather from a pterippus's left wing
- Three scales from an uprooter's tail
- A fang from the serpent who sleeps beneath the sea
- A tongue of a toad-like man from the Deepwood Swamp
- Tears from a weeping Squonk
- Steam from a teakettler's cry
- Flame from a firehawk's last breath

Endora skipped to the paragraph beneath the bulleted items. Her pulse rushed through her veins with the force of a raging river.

. . . the Blood Star's bond to only serve good will be broken. Its power will be yours to do with as you wish. It will bend to even the worst of intentions, enhancing your magic to cosmic levels. . .

"This is it. This is the curse I need to unlock the star's power!"

Her mind raced as she scanned the ingredients again. A feather from a pterippus—I wasted the last one from the astronomer's brute. She clenched her jaw at the memory of the winged-horse hobbled on Squally Peak. It had been all hers before that brat and her friends blasted Endora off the mountain and took the beast, and its owner, back to Mistford. It was the second time that little girl had defeated her—but it would be the last. I know where to find the pterippus. I can steal another feather. Her fingers twitched at the thought. I can sever its whole wing if I need to.

She pointed a sharp blood-red nail at the next item.

Scales from an uprooter's tail. Didn't Doug say that blasted lizard the brats had with them on Squally Peak lived with the astronomer too?

She couldn't believe her luck. It was too easy, like stealing a sinewy body from a freshly dug grave. Easier, in fact. And the tongue of a toad-like man? Her grin broadened. She had the perfect target—Arame, her traitorous ex-underling. She was certain he would be found cowering with his tadpoles in the Deepwood Swamp.

The lich pulled open the drawer of her desk, fetched a ballpoint pen and a notepad, and scribbled down the ingredients. She spun to face Doug and thrust the paper into his hand. "Take a couple of the guards and go to Mistford. Get everything on this list. You know where the pterippus and uprooter are."

Doug gripped the page with grimy fingers, his brows knit together in confusion. "Where am I spos'd ter find a teakettler? Or a fire'awk?"

"That's not my problem. Figure it out!" Endora rubbed her temple. "If you don't—"

"Yeah, yeah, yeah." Doug waved her off with a scowl. "I know, yeh'll put me in one o' yer portraits." Putrid mist seeped from his sleeves and swirled around him. "Yeh know, yeh got ter git a hold o' that temper. Me mum always said yeh catch more flies with toads." He paused and screwed up his face. "Or was it yeh catch more frogs with flies? I can never remember—"

"Just go before I shove you in a—"

"A frame. Got it. Good evenin', Ma'am." The mist thickened around Doug and with a sarcastic bow, he was gone.

"Stop calling me Ma'am," Endora hissed between her teeth.

She turned back to her desk and gazed at the star. It glistened in the glow of the book, promising her the future she had been fighting for for as long as she could remember. A life of power and revenge. The life she deserved.

Soon, I'll have the magic of the Blood Star. Then, I'll be able to do anything. She glanced in the mirror beside her desk, a gleam in her amethyst eyes. And then I can get revenge on that little brat, Fable.

Endora smiled. Her days of being confined to her mansion were coming to an end, an then it would be her great-granddaughter's turn to see what it was like to have her freedom stripped from her. With the Blood Curse, Endora could finally repay Fable for all the misery she and the rest of her family had caused.

You can't hide from me forever, child. I'll get the Blood Curse, and then we shall see who has all the power.

The Greenhouse

Come on, little bean. Grow!

Fable Nuthatch bit the side of her cheek, concentrating on the seed in the palm of her hand. A white light flickered within her ribs, warming her chest. Internally, she reached her heart towards the glow and shimmering green energy flowed through her and into the heart of the kernel. With a flash of emerald light, it split down the middle and a tiny plant unfurled from the jagged crack. Two round leaves stretched outward as if the seedling were yawning after an enchanted sleep.

A tray filled with a dozen green sprouts sat on the worn blue-chipped workbench in front of Fable. Early spring sunlight poured through the glass-paned walls of the greenhouse, bathing the young plants with soft yellow light. Another tray sat beside hers, neatly packed with dirt. But nothing had grown inside it yet. Fable's friend, Thorn, had planted that one the traditional way.

Fable gently tucked the new seedling into the loose

1

dirt and tamped down the soil around it. Shuffling foot-steps approached from behind her. She glanced over her shoulder to see Thorn towering over her.

The Folkvar girl peered at Fable's work with moss-green eyes set in her pale blue-grey face. It was hard to believe, but Thorn had grown even taller over the winter. If she didn't stop soon, she'd have to duck to miss the beams of the greenhouse rafters. Thorn pushed her waist-length copper braid, thicker than Fable's wrist, behind her shoulder. With her wide frame she looked as intimidating as ever, but Fable knew better. Her friend had a heart the size of the biggest mountain in all of Starfell.

Maybe even bigger than Grimm's. Fable glanced down at the tawny mastiff who lay in a spot of sun beside her. Even laying down, his shoulder reached almost halfway up the stool. With his droopy lips flutter-ing in time with his snores, he didn't look very fierce right now—but Fable knew that at the slightest hint of danger, he would leap to her defence.

Thorn narrowed her eyes at the tiny plants on the table. "Moira said you shouldn't use magic for every-thing. It's cheating."

Fable tucked a strand of her chin-length black hair behind her ear. "It's not cheating. I'm just giving this year's vegetable crop a strong start. Besides, how am

I supposed to hone my skills as a heart mage if I never use my magic?"

"You practice every day with Fedilmid," Thorn said, referring to Fable's mentor, the Fey Witch.

Fedilmid and his husband, Algar, owned Tulip Manor, the cottage where Fable, her Aunt Moira, her cousin Timothy, and her friends, Thorn and Brennus, had lived since last summer. Fable looked through the greenhouse window across the small meadow—green shoots barely poking through the soggy turf so recently revealed by melting snow—at the circular stone building with smoke curling from the chimney. With a start, she realized she was checking to see if Aunt Moira was coming out the sky-blue door of the cottage and heading to the greenhouse. She frowned. Let her come. Fable hadn't done anything wrong, no matter what Thorn said.

Thorn dug through the wicker basket that sat next to the planting trays. She pulled out a packet of seeds and held it up to her face. "Sugar pumpkins. These will be delicious in Algar's pies."

Fable reached for the packet, but Thorn raised it above her head.

Fable crossed her arms. "Come on. Let me sprout those too."

Thorn grunted and shoved the seeds into the pocket

of her canvas vest. She picked up the tin watering can from the bench and sprinkled water over both trays. After setting the watering can back on the table, she poked at one of Fable's sprouts.

"I don't think it's right to mess around with Mother Nature. Not if you can help it. Dad always said that forcing nature to work outside its cycles is an insult to the wisdom of the Earth."

"I'm helping Mother Nature," Fable replied. "I'm using the light inside me to boost her work. So she can be more productive."

Thorn pressed her lips together but didn't respond.

Grimm raised his head and let out a soft woof. His tail swished across the dirt floor as Brennus Tanager, Fable's other best friend and a rangy boy of fourteen years, entered the room with a stack of empty plastic trays in one hand and a pot containing a wilted sage plant in the other. He must have grown at least four inches over the winter, but even still, he barely reached Thorn's shoulder. Fable wondered if she would ever hit a growth spurt. She hated always being the shortest person her age. She glanced at her two tall friends. *Not that I'll ever catch up to them.*

"Doing more magic?" He peered at the new seedlings in curiosity, cocking a dark eyebrow. He set his burdens down on the table and gazed at Fable's work, a dimple forming in his russet brown cheek. He pushed his wavy black hair from his eyes and bent down to examine the tiny plants and nodded in approval.

"Nice job." He straightened. "I found this in the back room behind the rose bushes." He gestured to the withered shrub he'd just set down. "I thought you could help it with your magic-y finger wiggles."

Fable looked at the plant and ran her thumb over a dried brown leaf. *Poor thing must have been shoved in the back when we got the greenhouse ready for winter.* With protective sealing, mulch, and the help of Fedilmid's magic, the greenhouse had remained warm and humid all season. When the residents of Tulip Manor needed a break from the harsh weather, they merely needed to follow the frozen path from the cottage to the glass-paned building behind it. Even during the deadly cold snap in January, the greenhouse had remained filled with lush blooms and vivid green vines.

Brennus turned back to Fable's seedlings and gazed at them with admiration. "Fedilmid's going to be impressed."

Thorn crossed her arms over her chest. "And Algar will be impressed with my devotion to the natural way."

Brennus gave her a wry smile. "Sure. The natural, slower way."

"Sometimes, slower is better."

Fable wiped her dirty hands on the skirt of her purple knee-length wool dress, picked up her book bag from a nearby stool and slung it over her shoulder. She got down from her stool and glanced through the glass wall at the low sun. "Are Fedilmid and Algar back yet?"

The old couple had been gone for hours. After breakfast, they'd announced that they were going for coffee with Misty Hochberg. She lived in a cottage about half way to the Buttertub Tavern, which was a few hours walk through the Lichwood. They should have returned by now.

"I haven't seen them." Brennus worried at his lip. "Misty must be lonely there by herself since George disappeared. She probably needs the company."

Fable's heart pinched. Had Misty's missing husband been another one of her great-grandmother's victims? She blinked to banish the thought of the kindly farmer trapped inside a frame on the evil woman's wall. "Maybe they're extending the barrier. It's been quiet since last fall, but if they spotted one of Endora's undead . . ."

Thorn pulled a broken arrow shaft from the inside pocket of her vest. She twirled it in front of her, gazing at the pointed tip. "They could have found another arrow. Or, better yet, Orchid."

Fable stared at the arrow and subconsciously ran her hand over her book bag where the *Book of Chaos* rested. The wool felt warm beneath her fingers. The Collector radiated a pleasant heat when it was near the arrow or Brennus's magical guitar—the three objects that had been brought together by Endora's deadly powers.

"Now that the snow has melted, it should be easier to look for more clues. And maybe she'll come back," Fable said.

The arrow had belonged to Thorn's sister, who had appeared in the Lichwood in November. Blocked by the magical protective barrier around the meadow that Fedilmid and Aunt Moira had created, Orchid hadn't been able to see the people or the cottage of Tulip Manor. And before they could reach her, the Folkvar girl had been chased away by a hoard of Endora's undead guards.

Fable shuddered at the thought of the creepy hooded figures and their skeletal faces with rotting flesh hanging from their bones. They did whatever Endora said without question. There was no reasoning with them. Even Thorn, with all her strength, had been bested by them more than once.

Brennus leaned his elbows on the workbench next

to Thorn. "She's alive. I'm sure of it. Maybe Ralazar saved her, like my parents." Sadness tugged at the corners of his lips. "Fedilmid told me that warlocks often trick people into helping them. If he saw her at Endora's, I bet he made her a deal too. If I could ever get that guitar to work, we could ask my mom to keep a look-out for her."

Thorn grunted, still entranced by the arrow she spun in her thick fingers. "I wish the adults would let us search the forest. They've kept us under lock and key since that night Orchid appeared. I don't think I can take it much longer."

They were silent for a moment. Fable wondered if her friends' thoughts mirrored her own. Since that night, the woods had been quiet. Due to the heavy snowfall in the Lichwood, travel had been difficult. And after the scare of all those undead in the forest, Aunt Moira had put her foot down—there was no way anybody under the age of forty was leaving the protective barrier around Tulip Manor.

Fable couldn't help but wonder what her wicked great-grandmother had been doing all winter. *More than just biding her time, that's for sure.* After all, the evil lich had the Blood Star now. *At least she shouldn't be able to use it.* Fable hoped.

Fable shivered and wrapped her sweater tighter

around her. The last time they'd seen Endora had been that night on Squally Peak—after she'd tried to murder Fable for a spell that required her thirteen-year-old blood. The lich had been pulled into a writhing funnel cloud that had been created when Fable and Brennus joined forces and the magic of his mayhem-producing guitar and the *Book of Chaos* had merged together. The same twisted smoky tendrils that had attacked Timothy and dragged him through the book into a frame on Endora's wall had sprung from the objects' combined magic, snaring Endora and taking her to who-knows-where.

Had the two objects—originally Collectors created by Endora to trap souls in the portraits on her wall—transported her to one of those life-draining frames? If not, where had they brought her? Did Endora spend the entire winter plotting in her mansion? Or did the magic send her somewhere else?

At least she missed her chance to get my blood and work her spell. Hopefully, that means the Blood Star is useless to her.

Aunt Moira didn't believe for a second that Endora's defeat meant she was no longer a threat, missed chance or no. Fedilmid and Algar had gone to check her mansion several times since that night. The grounds lay quiet, and the house was dark. But that didn't mean

Endora wasn't inside, biding her time and growing stronger. The old crone loved the dark and despair of that place. If only Fable hadn't dropped the Blood Star during the fight with her great-grandmother last fall. If she had the Blood Star instead of Endora, then maybe the woman wouldn't be a problem anymore. Fable and her friends could go looking for Orchid without worrying about undead patrolling the forest, or protective barriers, or evil henchman hiding around every twist on the path.

Thorn broke the silence. "Are you going to heal it?" She nudged the terracotta pot that held the shrivelled sage towards her friend.

Fable gave Thorn a half-smile and raised her brow. "Didn't you just tell me that magic shouldn't be used for everything?"

Brennus snorted a laugh, then plunked down onto one of the stools at the workbench.

Thorn sighed. "Healing is different than forcing something to life before its ready."

"I didn't force the seedlings to life," Fable countered. She took a seat next to Brennus and pulled the potted plant in front of her. "I just nudged the spark of life into a flame." She ran her fingers over one of the crisp leaves. It crumbled under her touch. "This one might be hard to heal."

10

Thorn's face softened and she placed her hand on Fable's shoulder. "Do you want my help?"

Through their physical connection, Fable sensed the Folkvar's energy pacing like a caged zoo animal behind its enclosure. Fable cringed. She was a heart mage, which meant she could merge others' feelings and emotions with hers to strengthen her magic. But not every emotion was helpful. And sometimes, out of nowhere, her magic would snap to attention and latch onto the most intense feelings around her—no matter how negative the outcome.

"Fable?" Thorn gently squeezed her shoulder.

Fable shrugged off her friend's hand. "Thanks for the offer, but I better do this myself. Could you back up a few steps?"

Thorn's face fell, but she tucked the arrow into her vest and backed away. The current of agitation swept off Fable like a cloak blown away in a swift breeze.

Fable let out a breath. *That's better.*

She placed her hands on the brittle leaves of the sage. It was still green near the base, and Fable could sense its life energy throbbing as if it were looking for a lifeline to grab onto. She closed her eyes and concentrated on her earlier feelings of triumph, when the seedlings had stretched from the dirt into the sunlight. She reached for her light inside. Her fingers thrummed

11

as the green energy poured through them into the plant.

Easy peasy.

The dried leaves plumped and smoothed under her fingers, life radiating happily through the sage. Fable cracked an eye open, enjoying the warm glow of her magic mingling with the plant's energy. When it was just about filled to the tips with an emerald glow, a bright blue flash from outside the greenhouse caught Fable's eye.

She flinched, and the magic inside her cracked. Her heart hardened, smothering her spark. The plant shriveled beneath her hands, browning and shrinking to its base, looking even worse than when Brennus had first brought it to her.

She spun around, annoyed at the disturbance. "What's going on?"

"Something hit the barrier—" Thorn started.

"What do you mean, something hit the barrier?" She pictured a mob of undead storming the barrier and her heart froze. She swallowed the lump in her throat. Magic curled in her chest—fiery hot instead of its usual warm glow.

The bright blue light flashed again.

Thorn gasped and bolted from the greenhouse, leaving the door open behind her.

Grimm leapt to his feet with an anxious whine,

bumping into Fable's stool. She gripped the edge of the table to steady herself and looked at Brennus.

"What's she doing?"

Her friend slid down from his stool, his face tight with worry. "Something hit the barrier. I think it was an arrow."

Relief flooded over Fable. It wasn't a flash from an undead. *But maybe it was from was a Folkvar?*

"We'd better follow Thorn and find out." Fable jumped from her stool and followed her friend and the burly dog, but then hesitated at the door. She glanced over her shoulder at the dying sage on the workbench. A small thread of worry wormed its way into Fable's thoughts. *Another failure.* She gulped. *Why am I letting thoughts of Endora and her undead get to me—and my magic?*

She cringed, once again feeling the prick of the dagger tip at her throat while Endora's voice rasped in her ear. *Too late.*

Fable shook off the sense of dread. Now wasn't the time to get sucked into memories of that night on Squally Peak.

She had to be strong. Thorn needed her.

Fable hurried through the doorway and followed her friends into the late-afternoon sun.

Wayward Magic

Fable and Brennus raced over the dull grass, speckled with the first green shoots of spring, to the bottom of the hill where it met the magical barrier that hid Tulip Manor from the surrounding Lichwood forest. Grimm, their constant companion, loped along behind them.

Thorn already stood near the translucent barrier, squinting into the trees on the other side. When Fable reached her, the Folkvar girl muttered, "I'm sure an arrow hit right here. It must be hidden in the grass."

Brennus trotted up to Thorn's other side. He tapped the iridescent wall and a ripple of blue light spread from the point he touched. He peered into the long grass on the other side. "I thought I saw it too. At least, it sure looked like an arrow."

A rustling noise came from the trees. Quick footsteps approached. A familiar elderly couple appeared at the head of the trail, rushing towards the barrier. The silver stars of Fedilmid's navy blue robe twisted around him and Algar's wool sweater was covered with burrs and needles from the forest.

Fable's chest warmed at the sight of them. *Maybe they know what's going on.*

Fedilmid pushed the sleeves of his robes up to his elbows and raised his hands in the air. His grey brows knit together as he concentrated. It looked like he was staring straight at Fable and her friends, but she knew from his side, all he would see were the trees of the barrier spell illusion. He murmured something and a glistening crack, big enough for the men to slip through, appeared in the transparent wall.

Once they were inside the safety of the clearing, Thorn rushed up to them. "Did you see Orchid?"

Fedilmid gave her a tight look, then whirled to face the barrier. He began to chant in such a rush that the words blurred together. Blue energy flowed from his fingertips and poured into the open split in the enchanted wall, sealing it from the top down.

Algar hurried to Fable's side. Beneath his silver-streaked grizzled black beard, his mouth was set in a firm line, and his deep brown face glistened with sweat. "Fable, help Fedilmid seal the barrier. An undead is following us. We need to hurry."

An undead? Fable's pulse quickened. *What's an undead doing this close to Tulip Manor? Is Endora af-*

ter us again?

Fable swallowed, then took her place beside Fed-ilmid. She could ask questions later. Right now, she had to protect her home. Her family. Closing her eyes, she rubbed her hands together and drew in a deep breath.

When she reached for her magic, emotions swirled around her like a storm. She clenched her jaw, trying to focus and feel for the energy she needed. Threads of calm, presumably from Fedilmid, swam lazily through a whirlwind of anxiety that blazed out-of-control in and around her. She tried to cling to the old witch's quiet strength, but a swarm of fear gripped and pulled at her stream of magic as if trying to break it.

Fable looked at her mentor, her stomach taut. "I can't hold off these bad feelings."

Without taking his eyes off the magic pooling into the open space, Fedilmid took Fable's hand. He squeezed it softly, and his tranquility flowed into her like water breaking through a dam.

The tightness in her chest loosened, and she began to sing. She couldn't understand the words that rolled off her lips, but she didn't need to. They flowed from her as effortlessly as if she'd known them all her life. Perhaps she had. The important part was their mean-ing—safety and protection.

Bright sapphire-coloured energy poured from her

hands and mingled with Fedilmid's. The spell grew darker, dense and thick. It swelled and pulsed around them, radiating calm in the middle of the hurricane of emotion. The slice in the barrier began to fill at a faster rate—it was nearly half-covered now. The panic in the air eased.

Fable smiled through her song. When her magic worked like this, in rhythm with Fedilmid's and in time with the earth, everything fell into place. She felt strong and worthy. She felt *right*. She could do anything. Heal a plant and help her friends. Even defeating Endora would be easy if Fedilmid stood at her side.

Abruptly, a figure in a black hood lunged from the trees onto the trail, catching Fable off guard. It held a bow that was longer than Fable was tall. With one jerky movement, the creature pulled back the string and let loose an arrow. With a resounding *thwack*, it struck the split that Fedilmid and Fable were filling. A crack spidered from the spot where the arrow struck—a dark blue vein in the once-perfect shimmer.

A thread of panic surged through Fable and into her magic. Thoughts of undead swarming the forest like they did that night Orchid found the manor stormed through Fable. What if they got through? Her magic dimmed and flickered, nearly winking out.

Her voice cracked as she squeezed the old man's

hand. "Look out!"

Fedilmid's magic jolted so hard it caused Fable to stumble.

"Keep trying!" Fedilmid jerked his head back, then gathered his strength and directed their magic to the split in the wall. Fable followed his lead, leaning into her mentor's strength.

The figure nocked another arrow and yanked the bow's string, preparing to strike again. Its hood had fallen back from its face, and all Fable could see were those hollow, eyeless sockets staring at her from the grey bone of the skull.

Grimm snarled from behind them. Before Fable could react, he barreled past her and threw himself at the not-quite-full slit in the barrier. Thorn and Brennus scrambled after the dog, but he was too fast. He howled in frustration as he tried to reach the undead creature on the other side. Fable watched in horror as he lunged at the barrier again.

He's going to break it!

"Grimm. Stop!" A sudden terror broke through Fable's magic, and without thinking she threw her hands at the invisible wall. A burst of bright blue energy shot from her and hit the barrier at the exact same instant as Grimm.

The massive dog let out a strangled yelp and fell to

the ground.

Fable's heart slammed against her ribs and she froze, staring at the motionless dog. *No! What have I done?*

The undead lowered the bow and swivelled its head around as though looking for something, its gaze sliding over the group as if they weren't there. The slice in the barrier had been filled by Fable's outburst, hiding them from view.

Thorn and Brennus huddled around Grimm. He wasn't moving.

Horror seared through Fable. "Grimm!" She sprinted to his side and squatted beside the mass of brown fur.

Thorn stared at her from the other side of the dog. She placed her hands gently on his side. "He's barely breathing—but he's alive."

Brennus hovered over them, his eyes wide and his face drawn. "Fable, can you fix him?"

Tears slid down Fable's cheeks. Her precious Grimm rested with his eyes closed and his tongue hanging from his jowls. If it weren't for the rise and fall of his ribs, she would have thought he was dead.

Could she trust herself to heal him? Her heart lurched. *What if I injure him even more? Or worse . . .* Her next thought was so horrible she shook it from her mind as soon as it appeared.

The giant mastiff had been her protector, best friend, and comfort from life's terrible moments for over half her life. In return, she'd maimed him. And if she couldn't fix this, maybe even killed him.

Fedilmid appeared at her side with Algar close behind him. He kneeled next to her and placed a hand on the unconscious dog's head. His tense face softened and he gave Fable a reassuring smile. "He's okay. He took a good thump, but with a little help he'll be right as rain. We can fix this."

Guilt gripped Fable's throat like an icy claw, causing her to choke on her words. "I hurt him. I can't trust myself."

"It wasn't your fault. Accidents happen." Fedilmid's voice was kind, as if he understood what she felt. Maybe he did. "Would you like me to take the lead? You can join when you feel ready."

Fable swallowed a sob. She couldn't trust herself, but she trusted Fedilmid. She'd never seen him heal anything like this before but she had to let him try. For Grimm's sake.

"Okay."

Thorn took a step back and stood beside Brennus and Algar.

Fedilmid spread his hands over Grimm's shoulder

and side. He closed his eyes and began to hum. Gentle waves of soothing energy rolled across Fable and the injured dog.

Grimm gave a heavy sigh and licked his droopy lips.

It's working!

Fedilmid opened his eyes and looked at Fable. "With your help, he'll be healthy as a firehawk with a belly full of dew worms."

Fable pushed her worries aside. She placed one hand on Fedilmid's forearm and tenderly laid the other on Grimm's head. Her magic sprang to life and joined with Fedilmid's stream of compassion and joy. She let the old witch guide their power. Seconds later, Grimm's whole body radiated with a soft green glow.

His eyes popped open. With a joyous bark, he floundered to his feet, pushing Fable into Fedilmid's side.

"Grimm!" Thorn cheered.

Brennus punched the air. "He's alright!"

The dog cocked his head and gave them a confused look. With a grunt, he shook his entire body as if he were trying to wring himself free of his near-death experience.

Fable wiped the tears from her cheeks and beckoned to the dog. His tongue lolled out to the side as he lunged into her arms. Fable held up her hands to block his sloppy mastiff kisses, but it was no use.

She wiped the drool from her face and gazed into her dog's warm brown eyes. *He trusts me more than anything, and I almost killed him.* What would have happened if Fedilmid hadn't been there? Her heart splintered at the thought. Magic swelled within her chest.

Fedilmid chuckled. "Grimm, old boy! We're glad you're okay." He reached out to scratch the mastiff's ears, and in his delight, the dog swung his lion-sized head right into Fable's face.

Lost in her own grim thoughts, she let out a surprised squeak and her magic snapped. Pink glitter erupted from her hands and hit poor Grimm directly on his nose. He wobbled backwards onto his haunches, his eyes wide with shock.

And then, he sneezed, causing the loose skin of his jowls to flop nearly to his ears.

He sneezed again.

And again.

No! Dread seized Fable's thoughts. *What have I done now?*

Grimm gave one last violent sneeze and then froze, staring at Fable.

She cupped his face in her hands and rubbed his

floppy ears. "Are you okay?"

The mastiff responded with a hiccup. A bright pink bubble escaped his droopy lips and floated into the air. It burst with a loud *POP*.

Fable's heart dropped.

Algar, Brennus, and Thorn burst into laughter. Even Fedilmid, now on his feet behind Fable, struggled to hide his grin.

Grimm hiccupped again. This time a stream of bubbles poured from his mouth and surrounded his head in a chorus of popping noises. He shook his head and swung his accusing gaze to Fable.

She covered her mouth with her hand and let out a groan.

Thorn let out a bellowing laugh.

Brennus struggled to keep a straight face, but his eyes watered and a mischievous grin broke though. "It's better than the last spell you just did on him."

Algar tried to quiet them between his own snickers. "Alright, children, we best get up to the house. Moira is expecting us—"

"She's going to kill me!" Fable desperately rubbed Grimm's head as though she could wipe the magic away. "First I almost killed him and now I've turned him into a live bubble machine."

Fedilmid stroked his well-groomed beard. He

regarded the dog, who hiccupped rapidly and sent a stream of pink bubbles into the air.

"She will not. We'll get this fixed before she—"

"What in all of Starfell is going on down there?" Aunt Moira's shrill voice shot through the air. It came from the direction of the cottage. Fable turned to see her aunt march down the hill, waving a ruler above her head.

Fable's stomach dropped.

Thorn and Brennus's laughter softened into hushed giggles.

Fable stood and brushed the grass from her knees. "It was an accident. One of Endora's guards was at the barrier. Grimm tried to attack him."

"What?" Fable's aunt reached the group. Her flowing skirt twisted around her legs. Loose tendrils of frizzy hair escaped her high bun. "What do you mean—one of Endora's guards was at the barrier?"

"We handled it, Moira," Fedilmid said gently. "The barrier's up. We're safe."

Aunt Moira pressed her lips together, about to say more, but Grimm rubbed his head on her hip. She glanced down at him. He hiccupped and a spurt of glistening pink orbs gushed from his jowls.

Moira's brows shot up so high that Fable thought they would reach her hairline. "Why does your magic always go off on poor Grimm?"

Fable ignored her friends' snickers from behind her. "I don't know. It just does."

"He seems to have terribly rotten luck," Fedilmid said cheerfully. "Don't worry, Moira. We'll fix him up." He winked at Fable. "We always do."

Aunt Moira straightened her skirt and pushed a stray lock of hair from her eyes. "Well, best get on with it. I've got news from Mistford to share after you're done here."

A flamingo-coloured bubble floated near her head. With an annoyed glance, she popped it with the ruler. "We received a letter from Alice. I think you'd better come inside to hear it."

"A letter from Alice?" Brennus piped up. "Has she seen my parents?"

"No—"

Thorn's face lit up. "Or responded to my letter about the best method to grow basil?"

Brennus snorted. "Maybe she brewed up a potion to cure Fable's chaotic energy?"

Fable's face grew even warmer.

Aunt Moira folded her arms across her chest and gave the kids one of her familiar are-you-finished glares.

Algar shot the children a look. "Let her speak."

Once they were silent, Moira rested her gaze on Thorn. "Nestor spotted a Folkvar girl in Mistford. At the fairgrounds."

Fable's breath caught. *A Folkvar!*

"Orchid," Thorn said in a hushed voice.

Aunt Moira waved a finger at them, then started up the hill. "Come up to the cottage and I'll read the letter to you all. Timothy's waiting—very patiently."

Fedilmid and Algar fell into place beside her. Grimm bounded after them. A stream of pink bubbles trailed behind him.

Fable and Brennus started after the adults, but Thorn hung back. She peered through the barrier at the grass on the other side, then ran her hand over her vest where she kept her sister's broken arrow. "I thought it was Orchid, earlier." She glanced at her friends, her mouth tight. "I was fooling myself, wasn't I?"

"I thought it was her at first too," Brennus replied.

"We had no way to know it was an undead," Fable said.

Thorn looked at the forest with longing in her eyes. "Do you think Alice really could have seen her in Mistford? I mean, it could have been someone else. Maybe somebody from the mountain colony?"

A cold breeze swept through the clearing, rustling the budding branches on the trees behind the barrier.

26

Fable shivered. "Let's go see what her letter says."

"Maybe she has news about my parents too," Brennus said. There was a note of yearning in his voice. "It's been months. Their shop must have shifted to Mistford at least once."

"I bet it has," Fable agreed. Bound by the warlock Ralazar's curse, Brennus's parents were stuck managing the *Odd and Unusual* shop. It was unusual for more than just its wares—the magical store teleported around Starfell like a ball in the world's most erratic game of ping-pong. The Tanagers never knew where they would end up next.

Thorn led the way towards the cottage, and Brennus fell into step beside Fable. He tugged at her sleeve in a playful motion and gave her a sideways glance.

"Everything okay?"

Her breath hitched, but she nodded silently. *Other than the fact that I just about killed my dog.* But she couldn't talk about it. The thought of what she'd done was so horrifying that the words wouldn't form on her lips. She gave Brennus a weak smile.

He squeezed her arm affectionately but let the subject drop. "Last one to the cottage is a slimy webcap?"

Thorn's voice floated back to them. "You've actually been listening to my mushroom lessons."

"Nah, everybody knows what a slimy webcap is."

Brennus gave Fable a wink, then took off at a run.

"Hey!" Thorn bolted after him.

Grimm rushed from the cottage's sky-blue door to greet them. His booming bark was cut short by a hiccup and another mass of bubbles.

Fable's smile faded.

How could I be so weak? So thoughtless? After discovering she was a heart mage, she had thought her magic would fall into place. She'd assumed that it would be easier now.

Endora's haggard form from Squally Peak staggered before her, her hair singed and her lipstick smeared. A wicked grin broke over the crone's blackened face.

Fable pushed away the memory and her fear. *I have to stop thinking about this. I have to be strong. For my friends—my family at Tulip Manor.*

THREE

A Folkvar in the City

When Fable and her friends reached the circular cottage, Aunt Moira stood at the stove in the kitchen. She set a copper kettle on it and cranked the gas burner. Copper pots and pans hung above her head. Drying herbs dangled from a wooden rod above the sink, infusing the home with the fresh smell of lemongrass and thyme. Fable took a deep breath and the tightness in her chest eased. With stacks of old books, potted plants, and Fedilmid's porcelain figurines taking up every nook and cranny, Tulip Manor felt like home.

Thorn and Brennus joined Timothy at the long oak table in the dining area. He slouched in his chair, his face scrunched in concentration as he jabbed at the buttons of his handheld video game.

Grimm padded to the thatched rug by the fireplace in the living area, flopped down, and hiccupped a stream of sparkling bubbles into the air.

Timothy looked at the bubbles, then swept his gaze from the dog to Fable. "What did you do to him?"

Fable wrinkled her nose. "Why are you blaming me?"

"Of course it was you. It's always you." Her cousin set his game on the table. "Remember that time you floated him into the air like a parade balloon?"

Fable cringed at the thought of that day in the forest behind Rose Cottage, their home in Larkmoor, before they'd gone through the *Book of Chaos* and started their new life. "Never mind. Fedilmid and I will fix him."

Fedilmid emerged from the back room and took a seat across from Timothy. He gave Fable a sympathetic look. "Grimm might sleep it off. Let him relax and we'll see."

Fable took a seat next to the old man. She gazed at Timothy's tousled brown hair and the healthy pink of his freckled cheeks. It was hard to believe that it was only months ago that the eight-year-old boy was a shell of what he was now. Traumatized from his time trapped in a portrait on Endora's wall, terrors had taken over his sleep. Something as minor as a strong breeze could have sent him cowering to Aunt Moira's side. He still suffered from the occasional nightmare or headache, but he had regained his usual boyish energy. And his annoying little-cousin attitude.

Brennus picked up the game console from the table

and inspected it. "What are you playing now?"

"The first *Alien Invasion*." Timothy paused and looked at Aunt Moira. He raised his voice. "I've played it a million times. I could really use a new game."

Aunt Moira didn't respond, but the purse of her lips gave away the fact that she'd heard him. The kettle whistled. She turned to the cabinet above the counter and pulled out several mugs.

Fedilmid chuckled and clasped his hands on his knee. "How about a game of seeing how many dirty clothes you can pick up from your bedroom floor?"

Timothy groaned. "That's not a game. That's a *chore.*"

The front door swung open and Algar bustled inside with an armload of firewood. He plunked the wood down beside the fireplace, waved a few bubbles out of the way to give Grimm's head a scratch, then sat down on Fable's other side. He turned to the children.

"Are you ready to discuss the letter?"

Timothy's face lit up and he straightened in his seat. "It's from Alice! They've seen a Folkvar—"

Aunt Moira cleared her throat and strode into the dining area with two mugs of tea. "I told you not to read it." She raised a brow. "You didn't listen, did you?"

Timothy's ears turned bright red, but he couldn't hide his smile. "Sorry, Mom."

Aunt Moira gave him a disapproving look, set the tea in front of Fedilmid and Algar, and then retrieved a third mug for herself. She stood at the head of the table, cradling the mug in her hands.

"Well, now that we're all here, I'll share the letter with everyone."

She placed her tea on the table, then went to the shelf behind Brennus and picked up a stained brown envelope from between the cactus and azalea pots. She pulled out the letter and began to read.

"Dear residents of Tulip Manor, I hope this letter finds you well. Nestor and I have been busy preparing the inn for the Spring Festival and the start of the tourist season in Mistford. The garden has been planted and the cold boxes are bursting with herbs. Piper and Nightwind are feeling much better and miss you all. They say hello."

Fable's heart warmed at the mention of the pterippus and uprooter who had helped them on their mission to face Endora and locate the Blood Star. Without Piper, the fiery little lizard whose magic encouraged others to follow him, they never would have found Brennus' parents or Nightwind, the winged horse the lich had kidnapped from Nestor for its magic.

And, despite his help, I failed them all anyways. Fable deflated at the memory. She and Brennus may have defeated Endora that night, but the horrible crone had still won in the end. She had the Blood Star, the key component to her spell to strengthen her power— and possibly break the ties that held her magic trapped inside that mansion. *At least she didn't get a chance to use it on my thirteenth birthday like she wanted.*

Aunt Moira continued, "On a more serious note, Minister Hedgeway has still not replied to our inquiries about what they found at Endora's mansion. The city has been carrying on as if nothing happened last fall. There's been no sign of Endora or her henchman. But we're sure she's still alive and stirring up trouble."

Brennus cocked his eyebrow. "You think?"

Aunt Moira gave him a sharp look, then continued. "Nestor has found further information about the Blood Star's magic in one of his books that you may find interesting. I think it best to share it in person."

Fedilmid frowned at this, causing the whiskers around his mouth to twitch. Algar tugged at his frizzled beard.

Fable exchanged a glance with Brennus. What on earth could that mean? Endora had missed her chance to use the star's magic, hadn't she? Had she figured out another way to access its powers?

Aunt Moira kept reading. "In spite of all this, I do have some good news. Nestor and I saw a Folkvar as

33

we were walking by the festival grounds on our way to lunch. She was a tall, lanky girl with copper hair, and she carried a bow. I immediately thought of Thorn and her missing sister, but we lost the girl in the crowd before we could approach her."

Thorn sat upright, her eyes wide. "Orchid," she breathed.

Aunt Moira turned the page to read the back. "In light of all of this, we thought you might like to come to town for the festival. You are all more than welcome to stay at the Thistle Plum, free of charge. We miss your smiling faces, and would love to meet dear Timothy. The fair starts on April twelfth—"

Brennus let out a whoop. "That's in three days! We can visit my parent's shop—"

"We're going, right?" Timothy eyes were bright with excitement. "I want to see Mistford and the Thistle Plum."

"Let me finish." Aunt Moira held the paper in front of her nose. "The fair starts on April twelfth and runs to the eighteenth. You are welcome to come in advance. Warm regards, Alice and Nestor Serpens."

Fable's thoughts whirled with this new information. Did the Blood Star's magic survive when it, along with Endora, vanished through the portal created by the guitar and the book? And was there some way to get it back?

The story Thorn found at the library in Mistford had said the star wanted to do good. Fable had felt its pull. She even thought the star had fallen to help her. If she could get it back, maybe they wouldn't have to worry anymore. Using the magic from the star, they could find Orchid and maybe even break Brennus' parents' curse. They could stop Endora for good.

But what if Endora found a way to use it first? And how in Starfell were they supposed to get it back? She swallowed, her hands clammy.

"The Folkvar they saw has got to be Orchid, right?" Brennus jerked his head at Thorn, his wavy black hair falling into his eyes. "How many other red-haired Folkvars would be wandering around Mistford with a bow?"

Thorn's moss-green eyes were round as saucers. She ran her fingers over the end of her thick braid. "I can't think of any."

Timothy stood and knelt on his chair, his hands braced on the table. "We have to go. We have to find Orchid, visit Brennus's parents, and see Fable's house—"

"Children." Aunt Moira tucked the letter between the two potted plants on the shelf. She adjusted a pin in her hair, her mouth turned down in a look of worry. "It might be best if one of the adults goes first to make sure it's safe. If Endora and her henchman are in Mistford causing trouble—well, we don't know for sure—"

Fable's heart tensed. Her face burned as she gave her aunt a desperate look. "You can't be serious. We have to find out what Nestor has learned about the star. And find Thorn's sister!"

Fedilmid leaned forward and patted Thorn's hand from across the table. "Perhaps we should hear what Thorn thinks."

Thorn regarded Aunt Moira with misty eyes. "We don't know for sure that it's my sister, but I'd like the chance to find out. Orchid's out there, somewhere. She could be the only survivor from my colony. She could have information about what happened to the rest of them." Her voice quieted. "And she might not know about our parents yet. I have to find her."

Aunt Moira's face fell. She rounded the table and wrapped her arms around Thorn's shoulders. Her voice was high, in a tone that Fable recognized—her aunt was holding back tears. "Alright. We'll all go to Mistford together, dear. I was only thinking of your safety."

Thorn gripped Aunt Moira's arm. "Thank you."

Relief flooded through Fable.

Another trip to Mistford! She loved the magical city. The lights, the colourful houses, the clock that looked like the sun or the moon depending on the time, and her childhood home. And of course, all the wonderful shops and delightful treats. *Maybe we'll get to see Brennus's parents too!*

Timothy and Brennus high-fived, both of them grinning from ear-to-ear.

"Perfect!" Algar rapped his knuckles on the table. "We can take a look at Fable's house while we are there. I'd like to make a list of improvements that need to be done this summer before it's ready to move in."

My house! Fable's heart leapt as she thought of Eighteen Lilac Avenue. Fedilmid had taken Fable to see her childhood home the last time they were in Mistford. Even though it was in a terrible state of disrepair, she had fallen in love with its lilac hedges and faded lavender door. It was where she had started her life with two loving parents—before Endora had ripped it all away from her.

Now, thanks to Fedilmid, the old house was hers. And once it was fixed up, she and Aunt Moira and Timothy could live there. Maybe even Thorn and Brennus, as well.

"Wonderful idea, Algar," Fedilmid agreed. "Moira, do you think we could be ready to leave tomorrow?"

Aunt Moira cocked her head. "It'll be tight. I have books to pack, as I can't have the children missing any school—"

Brennus and Timothy both let out a groan.

Aunt Moira ignored them. "But I think we could make it work."

Fedilmid nodded. "Perfect. I'll send Alice a letter, express post." He wiggled his grey eye brows. "I've been meaning to fill her in on a new method of getting rid of peppermint mites. I read about it in the new issue of Druid's Digest. It's absolutely genius. You simply plant chocolate mint beside it. Apparently, mites have quite a hankering for cocoa."

"But what about the chocolate mint?" Timothy asked.

"It's for the mites. They need something to eat, after all."

Fable grinned. "Of course."

Thorn nodded her head. "Seems like the right thing to do."

Grimm, who was still laying on his bed, let out a long belch.

Fable spun in her chair to see two pink bubbles as big as basketballs burst above the dog's head.

She glanced at Fedilmid. "Do you think it's wearing off?"

Aunt Moira gave Fable a firm look. "Fix him."

Fedilmid stood from the table and motioned towards the door. "Let's take him outside and patch him up quick. I'll help you."

"Why can't we do it inside?" Fable asked.

Fedilmid eyed the pink drool that dangled from the dog's lips. It almost reached the wood-planked floor. "The spell I have in mind will empty his stomach. And unless you want to mop up pink slime . . ."

Fable's stomach lurched. "Got it. Let's go."

Grimm barked, but was muffled by another basketball-sized bubble floating from his lips. He heaved himself from the bed and followed Fedilmid and Fable to the door.

Fable slipped on her wool jacket and rubber boots. Everybody at the table had their backs to the entrance, laughing over something Brennus had said.

She leaned in close to Fedilmid. "What do you think Nestor has discovered about the Blood Star? And why couldn't Alice tell us in the letter?"

Fedilmid adjusted his robe, pulled a pair of deerskin gloves from his pocket, and put them on. "I suppose we'll have to wait to find out, won't we?" He paused and turned to the dining area. "This won't take but a few moments. Be sure to save us some of that berry cobbler." He shot Thorn a pointed look.

Fable grinned at her friends' and Timothy's giggles, but it faded when she caught sight of Aunt Moira and Algar exchanging a worried glance.

Something was up, and it had to do with Alice's letter. Fable had a sinking feeling that it was about the Blood Star. The hope she'd clung to that they might be safe from Endora because she had missed her chance to use the star faded. Whatever Nestor had found, it was just as likely that Endora could know about it too. If Fable's fears were true, unless they got the star back, they could be in as much danger now as before.

Fedilmid swung open the door and Grimm trotted outside, pink bubbles trailing in the air behind him.

"Coming, Fable?"

Fable swallowed her thoughts and followed him into the cool night air.

FOUR

Pink Slime

Fable's stomach squeezed as Grimm gave one final belch of pink slime onto the grass behind Tulip Manor. He hiccupped once, but no pink bubbles floated from his lips. Fable held her breath, waiting for another explosion of bubblegum-coloured goo, but no more came. The mastiff sat on his haunches and cocked his head as if asking himself if it was over.

"Good work, Grimm." Fedilmid walked up to the dog and scratched his ears. He and Fable had joined forces to heal Grimm, but when his stomach had started to heave, they'd taken a few steps back from the hacking dog—a few long steps back.

Luckily, their magic had worked.

Fable rubbed Grimm's head. In turn, he twisted his neck and licked her forearm, coating her jacket with slimy mastiff saliva.

"Ugh." She cringed and wiped her arm on the length of her coat. "I love you, Grimm, but we've got to do something about all that drool."

41

Fedilmid's lips twitched with a half-smile. "At least it isn't pink."

Grimm nudged Fable with his wet nose, then took off at a trot around the rounded wall of the cottage. Fable couldn't blame him for wanting to go back inside. Though the days had been warm and sunny enough to melt the mounds of winter snow, evenings in the Lichwood were still nipped with frost.

"Ready to go in?" Fedilmid asked.

Fable hesitated, thinking of her unconscious dog at the barrier earlier that day. Her fierce protector had been injured because of her and her uncontrollable magic. She glanced up at the old witch and her feelings boiled to the surface.

"Why can't I hold on to my magic? Every time I'm unhappy, I lose control. My magic hardens and darkness takes over." Her voice softened. "It happens every time I'm afraid."

Fedilmid ran his hand over his pointed beard, staring in the direction Grimm had gone. They heard him scratching at the door and somebody opened it to allow him inside.

After a thoughtful moment, the old man turned his gaze to Fable. "That's the hard part of being a heart mage. Your magic runs off emotions. But there's no shame in being afraid. You've been through some terrible things. It's only natural that you have some fear after all that. The key is to embrace those feelings and let the light inside you—that sliver of who you truly are—outshine the bad stuff that bogs you down. You can use your light to heal both your heart and your magic."

"Great," Fable said, more to herself than to Fedilmid. "So, until I can figure that out, I'll just keep killing plants and blasting my dog?"

Fedilmid chuckled and pushed his glasses up his nose. "You'll never be able to embrace your magic if you avoid your not-so-pleasant emotions. They will eventually erupt and demand to be heard." He paused. "If you're struggling, it's okay to accept help from others. On your own terms. You have a lot of support around you."

Fable kicked her toe in the dirt, smudging her rubber boot. "I've tried embracing my bad feelings. That's when my magic explodes."

And hurts everybody I love.

"It takes time. And some hard inner work." He gave her a sympathetic smile. "You'll get it. You're excellent at protection and healing spells. Perhaps you need to channel that energy. Allow your fear to energize you to do something good."

Fable bit her lip, still not sure how—or even if—she could do that. When her terror hit, it cracked as fast as a whip. Even now, her frustration writhed inside her, waiting to strike. The same way Endora struck with her evil powers.

For a moment, Fable was seated in her great-grandmother's nook across from the vile lich, whose words pierced her thoughts like a thousand tiny needles. *You haven't tapped into the darkness yet, but I can sense it in you. I can feel it flowing through your veins. You see, the same power runs through mine.*

"Fable?" Fedilmid's voice snapped her back to reality. "I can sense your feelings are running a little high right now. Care to use them with a simple clean-up spell?" He gestured to the remnants of Grimm's pink slime in the grass.

Fable shifted uneasily. She gave the goo a wary glance. "I've never done that before. I'm usually the one who makes the mess."

Fedilmid chuckled. "It's easy. Gather your magic, direct it to the mess, and imagine it being scrubbed away." He rubbed his chin. "I don't know why I didn't teach this to you ages ago. It would come in handy around here."

"You mean, if I learn this, Aunt Moira will pile more chores on my to-do list?"

"Just the dishes. And the floors. Oh, and washing the cupboards and walls, of course. Not too much."

Fedilmid's eyes glinted behind his spectacles. He scrunched his nose. "Maybe the laundry too."

Fable let out a laugh, feeling better. She rubbed her hands together, feeling a ball of energy grow between them. Magic pooled around her, lighting up with the playful energy of her and Fedilmid's banter. She pointed her hands at Grimm's gooey mess, guiding the iridescent wave as she imagined the slime fading away.

The drool began to evaporate into pink steam. Fable's pulse quickened. *It's working!* Her magic streamed seamlessly in a cheerful wave. No anger or frustration reared to grab hold of it.

Footsteps pounded on the path behind her, and the thought of an undead swooping down to drag her to Endora's mansion made her stomach clench. Before she could stop it, her magic sparked. It burst into one big ball of electric energy. With a *whoosh*, it smashed into the remaining slime and then winked out, leaving behind a charred circle where the drool had been moments before.

"Whoa!" came an awed voice from behind her.

Fable spun around to see Timothy in his too-big rubber boots and a jacket that reached his knees. He watched her with wide eyes, a look of amazement on his face.

She groaned, her irritation slamming into the pit of

her stomach. "Timothy! You scared me. I'm trying to learn a new spell."

His cheeks turned red. "Sorry, I just wanted to see what you were up to."

Fedilmid eyed the scorched grass. "Well, Grimm's mess is gone. But I think some more practice is in order before using that spell on the hardwood floor. Or the laundry."

Fable balled her hands into fists and shot Timothy a sharp look. "I would have done it right if you hadn't interrupted."

"You did it just fine," the old witch said. "Just a bit too much elbow grease. Next time we'll work on using less."

Timothy gave Fable a hurt look, then darted his gaze away from her. "Aunt Moira saved you some dessert. Better come get it before it's cold."

Fable swallowed. Guilt crept over her. "Sorry for snapping at you, Timothy."

"It's fine." He shrugged, avoiding her gaze.

What is with me today? I can't control my magic or *my mouth!*

"Let's go inside and get some of that cobbler." Fedilmid straightened and gestured towards the cottage. "We can practice cleaning spells later. Perhaps Alice would like some help around the inn."

Timothy snorted. "Does she want the Thistle Plum to burn down?"

Fable glowered at him but held her tongue. *I deserved that.*

She vowed to do better. It wasn't their fault that this darkness seeped through her. *Maybe Endora is right.* The woman's amethyst eyes flashed in Fable's mind. The same eyes as her own. *Maybe her darkness is inside me. But instead of strengthening me, it makes me weak.*

Secrets

Later that evening, Fable sat on the squishy couch in the living area of Tulip Manor. Her mother's journal lay open on her lap. She gazed at Thorn, who sat on the other end of the sofa, examining the broken arrow that had belonged to her sister. Brennus sat in Fedilmid's pink recliner with his guitar. The twisted vines that sprawled across its body stood out starkly against the blond wood. Timothy perched on the arm of the chair, watching in fascination as Brennus fiddled with the tuning keys.

Sprawling in front of the fire, Grimm, yawned and licked his chops, then let his head drop onto the woven rug with a *fump*. He was back to his old self with no sign of his earlier trauma. A lump formed in Fable's throat at the thought of her unconscious protector. How close had she been to killing the faithful mastiff?

Endora's vicious smile flashed inside her thoughts. It was as if her memories were mocking her—as if the phantom of her great-grandmother was pushing at the

48

seams of corruption inside her heart, fraying them until they tore.

What would they all think, if they knew what was happening inside me? Fear and anxiety bubbled beneath her surface almost constantly, but she'd been keeping it hidden. *They would think I'm a baby. And never trust me again.*

The adults had gone outside to check the barrier, as they did every evening. Since last summer, Fable had often joined them at Fedilmid's request. As her magic grew, he'd been trusting her more and more with the daily tasks around Tulip Manor. Tonight, however, she was not invited.

Probably a good thing. Fable picked at a loose thread on the quilt across her lap. *I'd probably kill us all by accident—if my magic even worked.*

Thorn tapped the head of the splintered arrow against the palm of her hand, catching Fable's eye.

The Folkvar girl glanced at her and stopped fidgeting. "How are you feeling? After what happened—"

"Fine." Fable's tongue stiffened with the lie. She swallowed. "Fedilmid helped me with Grimm."

"What did he say?"

About what? Fable wanted to snap at her friend. She took a breath. *No. She's just trying to help. It's not her fault that I can't deal with my magic.*

49

"Oh, you know. Just stuff about embracing the light inside me and letting it shine through the darkness."

"Seems like good advice."

Thorn returned to fidgeting, spinning the broken arrow between her fingers. It was another mystery in their never-ending list of things that didn't make sense—the weapon shouldn't have been able to get through the barrier. Nothing should be able to. But nonetheless, that arrow had been embedded in the front door of the cottage. And Orchid had clearly heard Thorn's cries.

Brennus strummed the guitar. A gust of smoke puffed from the sound hole. He scowled, batting at the smoke to waft it away. Like the *Book of Chaos*, the guitar had once been enchanted by Endora. It had transported Brennus's parents into a deadly portrait on the wall of her mansion—a portrait she used to steal the life from her victims. The Tanagers had managed to escape, but they had paid a hefty price for it.

Later, Brennus's mother had figured out how to contact Fable with the instrument. When she scribbled messages on its body, they would appear inside the *Book of Chaos*, the vine-covered book Fable never let out of her sight. Mrs. Tanager had left them clues about the Blood Star and had even drawn Fable a map to where it would fall. But since Brennus had been given the guitar, there had been no new messages in the book. No more maps or clues or anything about the Blood Star or Endora.

Timothy coughed, waving his hand in front of his face to clear the air. "Try the knob beside that one."

Brennus cast him an annoyed look. "They're called *tuning keys*. And I'm not touching that one again. Last time, it screeched like a boiling tea kettle. It took me forever to get it to stop." He let out a frustrated sigh. "If only I had magic. I made the guitar work once. Why can't I do it again?"

"Keep trying," Fable urged him. "I'm sure you'll get it. Maybe one of Fedilmid's books would help?"

Brennus scowled. "I've read all his books with portal magic in them and haven't found anything about instruments that can zap people all over Starfell."

The young teen hadn't been able to make the guitar do much since their battle on Squally Peak. At least, not anything useful. He'd been playing with it all winter, trying to astral project the way his mother did, desperately hoping to connect with them and figure out how to track the store they were bound to.

But all he'd been able to do was produce dragons made from steam and create brilliant rainbows that burst from the sound hole. Once, he had filled the cottage with an explosion of confetti. That had been Aunt Moira's least favourite trick. Fable would never forget the sight of her aunt being showered with tiny dots of sparkling rainbow paper. They still occasionally found bits of confetti in the couch cushions.

Fable turned her attention back to the journal and tapped her finger on the page before her. She had read through Faari's notes so many times that she knew many of the passages by heart. She could recite what wormwood, cone flowers, and chamomile would do when mixed as a tea or broth—get rid of parasites, ward off colds, lull you to sleep. She had memorized her mother's intricate botanical drawings and could recognize faari blossoms, elder berries, and fireweed on first sight. It was all useful information, but there was nothing about the Blood Star. The only hint was the torn page stub at the back with word fragments reading, *The Bl— Curse.*

"It may not even be about the Blood Star at all," Fable murmured to herself. She blew at a stray tress of hair that hung in her face, then closed the book.

Thorn gazed at the arrow twirling between her fingers, deep in thought.

She must be thinking about Alice's letter.

"Are you excited to go to Mistford and find Orchid?" Fable asked her.

Thorn shrugged and continued to stare at the arrow, its metal tip glinting in the firelight as it spun.

"I hope we find Orchid, but I'm not exactly excited about the festival and mobs of people." She wrinkled her brow. "I haven't forgotten what people think about Folkvars there. Remember what happened at Madam Mildred's?"

Fable grimaced. She, Brennus, and Thorn had been in the educational supply store looking for school items, and a cantankerous shopkeeper named Clarice had tried to kick Thorn out, just for being a Folkvar. "Not everybody shares Clarice's opinion. I won't let her get to you again."

Brennus glanced up from the guitar, letting his hands relax against the instrument. "She's an old bat, anyways. She hates all kids."

Thorn placed the arrow on the circular lamp table beside her with a pained look on her face. "I just hope Alice is right—that the Folkvar they saw really is Orchid."

"If it's not Orchid, who else could it be?" Timothy asked.

Thorn shrugged. "The Greenwood Clan isn't the only Folkvar colony in Starfell. There's another group in the Windswept Mountains. It could be somebody from there."

"Do they visit the cities much?" Fable asked.

"About as often as Greenwood Folkvars do. Which

is to say, not often." Thorn gazed into the flickering flames in the fireplace. "Even if she's not Orchid, I'd still like to meet her. It'd be nice to see another Folkvar. Somebody who understands what it's like to be an outcast."

Fable reached across the couch and patted Thorn's arm. "You're not an outcast. You're our friend."

Brennus propped the now smoke-free guitar against the side of his chair. "Yeah, we've got your back."

Timothy nodded. "Always."

Thorn gave them a tight smile and rubbed the back of her neck. "Thanks. I know that. It's just not the same."

There was a moment of quiet as they contemplated this. They had looked around in Endora's mansion last summer when the old lich had kidnapped them. There'd been no sign of Orchid—only Thorn's poor parents, frozen and lifeless in a frame on Endora's wall. Where had Orchid been all this time since she and Thorn were separated?

Brennus broke the silence. "What do you think Nestor has discovered about the Blood Star?"

Thorn picked up the arrow again and ran her fingers along the shaft. "Whatever it is, it must be important, or Alice would have told us in the letter. She obviously didn't want anybody else to read it."

"She was probably scared Endora would find it." Fable's chest tightened. "Just imagine what could happen if Endora found a way to unleash the star's power." *Or if she already has.*

Timothy let out a soft whimper at the mention of their great-grandmother. "Do you think she's strong enough to do that?"

Fable shifted uneasily. "She was able to summon a windstorm strong enough to put out a raging fire. Her mansion strengthens her, and so do the people she captures. Who knows how many more souls she's been stealing life from?"

Timothy stared at Fable as if there were a ghost behind her, his mouth gaping open.

"You don't look so good," Brennus said to the younger boy. "Maybe you should go to bed?"

Timothy swallowed, and for the first time that evening Fable noticed the bags beneath his eyes. As happy and vibrant as he'd been these last few months, he was still grappling with the trauma of his time on Endora's wall. *I should be more sensitive to him. But doesn't he deserve to know the truth?*

Timothy pressed his lips together, looking torn between staying and fleeing the conversation. He slumped his shoulders. "I am tired. And we have to get up early tomorrow."

He wished everybody good night and slunk from the room, a nervous hop in his step.

"Good night," Fable called after him. "We won't be long."

Brennus waited until Timothy had gone into their makeshift bedroom at the back of the cottage and closed the door, then leaned towards his friends. "I overheard Aunt Moira and Fedilmid talking yesterday in the greenhouse. They didn't know I was there at first. They said something about a Blood Curse."

Thorn pointed the arrow at Fable's notebook. "Like in Faari's journal?"

"What did they say?" Fable asked.

Brennus scratched his ear. "Well, I didn't hear much. After I accidentally knocked into one of Fedilmid's pink-leaved things—"

"Begonia," Thorn said.

Brennus wrinkled his nose. "What?"

"Begonia," Thorn repeated. "Pink silvery leaves? He's growing fairy begonias this year."

"Anyways," Brennus said, shooting her a perturbed look. "Before they heard me, Fedilmid said he'd been talking to Nestor about the star. I don't think Alice's letter is a surprise." He flicked his gaze from Thorn to Fable. "Moira mentioned your mother's journal. She said something about a curse."

Fable clenched her fingers on the fabric of the quilt across her lap. "She told me she didn't know what the missing pages could be about. And Fedilmid said he had no idea, either."

Brennus's brown eyes glinted in the firelight. "It sounds like they're trying to find out."

"Why wouldn't they tell me that?" Anger rose in the pit of Fable's stomach. "We're supposed to work together. That star, and that story, they affect me. I have a right to know."

"Maybe they don't want to tell us until they know for sure," Thorn said.

Fable closed her eyes, her fists clenched on her lap. She wanted to march outside right now and demand answers from her aunt and Fedilmid. Magic ballooned in her chest, pushing against her ribs.

Her breath hitched. *Calm down. The last thing I need is to lose control. Again.* Besides, there had to be a reasonable explanation. She should just ask them tomorrow about it. Maybe Brennus had misunderstood.

The front door to the cottage opened and Aunt Moira bustled inside. She took off her jacket and hung it in the overstuffed closet in the entry-way.

"Oh, children," she said, huffing as she kicked off her boots, "it's getting late. You should have been in bed an hour ago. We must be up early tomorrow. Have you all brushed your teeth?"

"Yes," Brennus and Thorn said at the same time.

Thorn tucked the arrow into her vest and stood. Brennus picked up his guitar and did the same, yawning as he said goodnight. He shambled off to the makeshift bedroom at the back of the cottage. When Fable didn't move, Thorn raised a questioning eyebrow.

"I'll be there in a minute," Fable said.

Thorn glanced at Moira, who was now scurrying around the kitchen gathering dried herbs and baking supplies. The Folkvar nodded and followed Brennus, ducking beneath the doorframe before she disappeared into the tiny room.

Fable pushed the blanket from her lap and stood from the couch. She looked at her aunt. "Could we have a talk before bed?"

Moira glanced at the cuckoo clock that hung on the wall beside the fireplace. "Can it wait until tomorrow? I have a lot of packing to do. Fedilmid and Algar are in the greenhouse making a list of supplies we need to pick up while we're in the city."

She opened the pantry and tapped her chin.

"We'll need to bring some sort of the snack for the drive." She paused. "Fable, would you double-check Timothy's bag to make sure he packed his socks? He always forgets something."

Fable slid her mother's journal into her star-spangled book bag and nestled it next to the *Book of Chaos*. "I'd like to talk now."

"I'm going to be up all night packing for our trip. Are you sure this can't wait?" She spied what she was looking for in the pantry and reached for it.

Fable slung the strap of her book bag over her shoulder. "Fine. But tomorrow at the Thistle Plum I'd like to talk to Nestor about the Blood Curse."

Aunt Moira paused with her hand in mid-air grasping a tin of nuts. She turned towards Fable, her jaw tight. "A blood curse? Where did you get that idea?"

"A little firehawk told me," Fable shot back.

Aunt Moira rubbed her temple and closed her eyes, resting the nuts against her stomach. "Alright. We'll have a chat with Nestor. Alice did say he's learned more about the star. I have no idea what kind of curse you're talking about, though." She opened her eyes and gave Fable a firm look. "But first, we need to visit Sergeant Trueforce and tell him, in person, about what happened at Squally Peak."

Fable's neck stiffened at the mention of the police sergeant in Mistford. He had been less than helpful the last time she and Fedilmid had approached him about Endora. In fact, he had blown them off completely.

"He didn't believe me last time," she said. "Why

would he now?"

Aunt Moira tossed the tin of nuts into the box at her feet. "Because she's grown stronger. What happened on Squally Peak, that was very serious."

Fable snorted. "I know. I was there."

Aunt Moira's voice grew higher. "You could have been killed. It's the police force's job to protect the people of Starfell. It's time they stepped up and took this seriously."

"How are we going to make them?"

Aunt Moira looked at Fable with a determined gaze. Her expression reminded Fable of Grimm when he was intent on chasing a rabbit.

Her aunt lifted her chin. "I'll come with you this time. He won't be able to kick me out of his office."

Fable swallowed. That might be true. Trueforce may have been able to brush off an old man and a little girl, but she couldn't imagine anyone dismissing her aunt so easily. Moira had years of experience dealing with cantankerous old men while working at the nursing home in Larkmoor. She could certainly handle the patronizing police sergeant.

Aunt Moira motioned towards the door of the bedroom. "Now, off to bed. Goodnight, Fable."

"Good night, Aunt Moira." Fable paused at the door and cast a glance over her shoulder at her aunt, who muttered under her breath as she rummaged for more snacks.

This trip to Mistford would be different than the last. With a headstrong Aunt Moira, maybe a trip to see Sergeant Trueforce would go better. Maybe he would finally listen and be able to stop Endora before she caused even more destruction.

The sudden thought of her injured dog caused her stomach to cramp.

Maybe they'll have to stop me before I cause any more destruction too.

The Pterippus Riders

Fable woke the next morning to the sound of somebody banging around in the kitchen. She rubbed her eyes, exhausted from her restless sleep, and swept her gaze over the makeshift bedroom. She was alone. Other than their untidy blankets, her friends' cots were empty.

She forced herself out of bed and pushed through the old wood door into the kitchen area. Sunlight hit her face, and the sound of splashing water met her ears. Fable squinted and Aunt Moira came into focus. She stood at the sink, vigorously scrubbing the pan from the previous night's roast.

Fable yawned and scratched the back of her neck. "Morning."

Aunt Moira kept scrubbing, sloshing soapy water up to her elbows. "Good morning, Fable."

Fable peered into the box sitting in the doorway of the pantry. It was filled with granola bars, oatmeal, and bags of various herbs. She glanced at the overcrowded front entrance. Half a dozen suitcases were stacked beside the door.

"What do we need all this for? We're only going for a week. And the Thistle Plum has food." Fable pushed a tangled lock of hair away from her face and tucked it behind her ear.

Aunt Moira wrinkled her forehead as she sponged the bottom of the pan. "The Serpins are kind enough to let us stay, using rooms they could be renting out. The least we can do is bring some food and help them around the inn. Besides, they'll be busy with guests for the spring festival. Algar and I can do some cooking."

Fable grabbed one of Algar's fluffy cranberry muffins from the glass jar on the counter. "Where is everyone?"

Aunt Moira let the pan slip down into the dirty dish water and jerked her elbow towards the front door. "Outside, fawning over the pterippus."

What? Fable nearly choked on her muffin. After swallowing her mouthful, she spoke. "Nightwind? Here?"

"Yes, dear." Aunt Moira waved her soapy hand towards the door. "Alice must have been reading Fedilmid's mind. Nightwind showed up here shortly after sunrise. Go see for yourself."

Fable shoved the last bite of the muffin into her

mouth and sprinted to the door. Hastily, she pulled her rubber boots on over her pajama bottoms, then ran outside to join her friends.

A winged horse stood on the lawn of Tulip Manor. He arched his neck, showing off the grey hairs peppered throughout his ebony coat. His wings, folded against his side, were so white they looked like porcelain in the morning sunshine. He wore a leather harness that held a wooden rack on his back. Saddle bags hung across his withers and over his shoulders.

Brennus, Thorn, and Timothy crowded around him. Brennus's guitar was already strapped to the harness. Grimm sat in front of them all, his club-like tail wagging back and forth as he gazed at what he must have thought was another huge dog. Fable was sure he'd never seen a horse before, much less one with feathered wings.

She jogged towards the group, slipping and sliding in her floppy boots on the dewy morning grass. Nightwind perked his ears towards her as she pushed by Brennus and held out her hand. The horse nuzzled her palm with his velvety black nose.

"Nightwind." Fable rubbed his face beneath his shaggy forelock. "What are you doing here?"

Thorn rocked back on her heels and gave Nightwind a look of admiration. "Alice and Nestor sent him.

He came with a note tucked inside one of the bags on his harness. He's here to help us get our things to the van."

Fedilmid and Algar kept their rusted old vehicle parked near the Parting Road, the dirt roadway that separated the Burntwood Forest and the Lichwood. It led to the two major cities in Starfell. Stonebarrow was in the north. Their destination, Mistford, was in the south.

By foot, the van was a few hours' walk. Fable hadn't been looking forward to the hike through the forest with all the luggage Aunt Moira was determined to bring. It was just like Alice and Nestor to think of that and send their beloved pterippus to help.

Timothy ran his hands over the soft leather of Nightwind's harness. He pushed his too-long bangs away from his eyes. "Maybe once he's moved our things, he can give some of us a ride to the Thistle Plum."

Fable scratched the pterippus's neck. "Only if we ask him nicely."

"How about it, Nightwind? Would you like to give me a lift to Mistford?" Timothy asked.

Nightwind snorted and shook his glossy mane.

Brennus narrowed his eyes at Timothy. "Why do you get to ride him?"

"Because you've already had a ride," Timothy

replied. "When he brought you home from Squally Peak."

Algar's gravelly voice sounded behind them. "I think you'd better ask your mom first."

The old man was carrying a canvas drawstring sack from the house. Brennus and Timothy scrambled to move out of his way.

"Hello, Nightwind, old boy. How goes it?" Algar murmured. He unclasped the buckle on Nightwind's left shoulder bag and slid the canvas sack inside it. "I hope you're taking good care of Nestor."

Nightwind craned his neck and pressed his head against Algar's arm. Algar scratched behind his ear, and the pterippus's lips quivered. With a gleam in his liquid brown eyes, he gave Algar's sleeve a nibble.

"Hey, now, you silly beast." Algar pushed the creature's nose away. He pulled a small carrot from his pocket and handed it to Fable. "Hold your hand flat. That way he won't mistake your finger for a carrot."

Fable did as he said, offering the creature the carrot. Nightwind sniffed the vegetable, his muzzle like velvet on the palm of her hand. He twitched his lips, then scooped up the carrot and crunched it down.

"You never have treats in your pocket for us," Brennus said.

"You all get enough treats." Algar buckled the saddle bag and gave it a pat. "And you don't work near as hard as Nightwind does."

The door to Tulip Manor opened and Aunt Moira bustled outside with a wooden box so tall she could barely peek over the top of it.

Brennus jogged to her side. "I've got it, Moira."

"Thank you, Brennus." Aunt Moira let him take the box. "Please have Algar help you load it onto Night-wind's back. It's heavier than it looks."

Brennus went to the horse's side, and Algar grabbed the other side of the box. Nightwind lowered his wings. The gangly teenage boy and the old man heaved the box onto his back.

"I'll show you how the buckles work," Algar picked up one of the straps that hung from the rack. "Back in our day, we used this contraption countless times on this bravest of steeds. Didn't we, Nightwind?"

The horse heaved a sigh.

Timothy looked at his mom. "Do you think, after these boxes are loaded into the van, that some of us could ride Nightwind to Mistford? If he's okay with it?"

Aunt Moira pressed her lips together. "I don't know. He'll already have to make several trips to get the luggage and all of us safely to the clearing. I wouldn't want to tire him out."

Nightwind nickered and pawed the ground, as if insulted by Moira's words.

Algar chuckled. "Nightwind can handle it. He has to fly back to the Thistle Plum anyways. Besides, Timothy weighs less than these boxes."

"And I'll ride with him," Fable said. "Then he won't be alone." She glanced at her friends. "I mean, if that's okay with Brennus and Thorn."

Thorn backed away from Nightwind and held up her hands. "I'll ride in the van."

"I didn't really want to ride him all the way to Mistford anyway." Brennus patted the horse's neck. "No offense. Last time we went for a ride, I almost threw up."

Nightwind snorted.

Brennus rubbed the pterippus's forehead. "It's not you. It's the altitude."

Algar tightened the last strap over the box and wiped his hands together. "I'll pass on the long ride, as well. My old joints haven't been the same since last time."

"Please, Mom?" Timothy pleaded.

Aunt Moira hesitated, looking at Timothy's bright expression. She tucked a stray lock of hair behind her ear, then wrapped her arm around Timothy's shoulder. "Okay." She looked at the horse. "I trust you, Nightwind, to take care of my children. Stay within view of the van the entire drive. And straight to the Thistle Plum. No stops."

"Awesome!" Timothy let out a whoop and punched the air.

Fable grinned and twisted a strand of Nightwind's mane in her fingers. She tucked herself close to his neck and wrapped her arm beneath it. "Looks like it's me, you, and Timothy."

"Only if Fedilmid agrees," Aunt Moira cut in.

"He will," Fable replied. She knew he would.

Fable tightened her grip around Timothy's waist. Nightwind swooped over the field below, which was a mixture of brown and green with the new grass shoots popping up. The trees that dotted the landscape were laden with shiny green leaves and pink buds, just waiting for warmer weather to burst forth with blooms. Wind rustled through her hair, and cold air brushed against her cheeks. She let out a shriek of delight as the horse sped downward, his wings flattened over the children's legs.

Timothy whooped as Nightwind extended his wings and beat them gently to rise out of the dive. The boy had the horse's mane twisted securely in his fingers and his feet lodged tightly in front of the pterippus's wings.

Below them, the robin's egg blue van rumbled over the dirt road that snaked between the hills. It carried the other residents of Tulip Manor, including what Fable was sure to be a bickering Thorn and Brennus. She could almost hear them now, arguing over which shade of red the road was. Or perhaps the best flavour of ice cream at the famous Drippity Cone in Mistford.

Fable's heart soared with Nightwind's gentle rise. The last time she'd ridden the pterippus after their escape from Endora on the mountaintop, the ride had been much less enjoyable—rushed, cold, and in the dark. Far more uncomfortable than this easy frolic through the cool breeze.

Nightwind straightened his path and the bright colours of the homes and buildings of Mistford appeared on the horizon. The familiar magical clock sat above the town at the top of its tower, shining like the midday sun.

"There it is," Fable said in Timothy's ear. "Mistford! The city of hearth, home, and magic. At least, that's what Fedilmid says."

Timothy clutched Nightwind's mane tighter with one hand and pointed with the other. "You can see the fairgrounds!"

In the distance a bright green Ferris wheel poked out from the city rooftops. Beside it, a large red and white tent dominated the festival grounds. It looked big enough to house a whole herd of pterippi. Maybe even a few giraffes, or one of those giant three-headed dogs Brennus had told her about. *A cerberus, I think he called them?* Fable could only hope.

Soon, they were flying over the city. The blur of colours became ornate brick homes with slate roofs and intricate iron fences. They glided over houses of bubblegum pink, sapphire blue, and parakeet green.

Timothy craned his neck to glance at Fable. "Which one's your house?"

Fable squinted, searching for Lilac Avenue. "The tiny one with the lavender door. We can't see it yet."

The rusted van beneath them was soon lost in the crowd of vehicles on the cobblestone streets below.

"Do you think we could check out the festival grounds?" Timothy asked.

Fable squeezed her arms tight around his sides. "I don't know if it's a good idea."

Aunt Moira wouldn't like it. She had been firm that they were to go straight to the Thistle Plum. No stops for any reason. She'd even insisted Fable wear one of Fedilmid's oval yellow speaking stones—a magical communication device he'd invented—around her neck, in case of an emergency.

The Ferris wheel loomed ahead of them like a rounded mountain on the skyline. They were close enough now to see the colourful bucket seats swaying in the wind.

A few minutes wouldn't hurt, would it? Her aunt might not even notice if they were quick enough.

"Let's go," Fable decided. "What do you say, Nightwind?"

The pterippus circled towards the festival grounds. Fable had never been to a carnival before. At least, not one like this. Larkmoor had a small harvest festival every year, but the biggest ride they had was a merry-go-round that had straps to hold riders in place. Boring, safe, and ordinary. Just like the town itself, cut off from the magic of Starfell by the Windswept Mountains.

Nightwind dove until he was flying just above the peak of the striped big top. Beside it, smaller tents and booths sat in straight lines in varying stages of setup. Games with targets were half-unpacked, and partially erected canvas structures speckled the grounds, some with signs and some without.

Timothy jerked his head towards a line of empty cages that sat alongside the big top. Some were large enough for an elephant and others were too small for even an uprooter. "Do you think there's a petting zoo?"

Fable snorted. "From the size of those cages, more like a monster zoo." She paused. *Maybe it actually is a monster zoo!* If there was anything she had learned about Starfell, it was to never underestimate the kind of magical creatures that lived there.

"Let's check out the sporting tent!" Timothy said.

Nightwind flew closer to the billboard sign in front of the stadium-sized structure.

Fable read some of the events listed in the small print on the sign. "Fencing, jousting, and archery." *Archery! That sounds like something Orchid would like.*

"Thorn could enter the strength competition. Just imagine—" Timothy broke off when a knight in shining metal armor emerged from the tent's entrance. "Wow! He must be one of the competitors."

Something tugged at the back of Fable's mind. That armour was familiar, with its smooth lines and polished helmet that glinted in the sunlight. But she couldn't quite place it. *Maybe he looks like one of the knights from our story books at Rose Cottage.*

She glanced at the sun clock that overlooked the city. It was time to go, before Aunt Moira started to fret.

"We better go—"

She broke off when the knight flipped the visor of

his helmet and glanced up at them with familiar dark eyes.

Her breath caught in her throat.

Before she had a chance to call out, the knight's face twisted into a scowl, and he disappeared inside the tent.

Timothy's spine stiffened. "Was that—"

"Sir Reinhard," Fable choked on the words. "I'm sure of it!"

A voice came from the sunshine-yellow stone that hung from Fable's necklace. "Children? Are you almost here?"

Thankfully, it was Fedilmid and not Aunt Moira.

Fable grasped the stone in her palm, her heart still racing from the sight of the knight who had helped them escape Endora's mansion. "Yes, we're close now."

"All right. Hurry up then, we don't want Aunt Moira on the chase for you."

"We'll be right there." Fable tucked the stone beneath her jacket. She tugged on the winged-horse's mane. "We'd better go to the inn, Nightwind."

The pterippus gently flapped his wings and turned towards his home.

After Fable and her friends had rescued Timothy from Endora's mansion, Sir Reinhard had bought them time to escape. He'd been trapped in a portrait above the desk in Endora's library, and had pulled Endora into the frame in time for Fable to fix the glass and lock her inside. The children had fled through Arame's portal before they'd found out if Sir Reinhard escaped too, but now, here he was. She smiled, happy that they hadn't abandoned him to his doom.

But what's he doing in Mistford? Her mind raced. *And why did he glare at us? Did he truly escape from Endora—or has she enslaved him the way she did Arame?*

As Nightwind glided over the rooftops in the direction of the Thistle Plum, Fable couldn't dismiss the uneasy feeling that something strange was going on.

We'll be back tomorrow. I'll find Sir Reinhard then and learn the truth.

Now to talk to Nestor and find out what he knew about the Blood Star.

SEVEN

The Blood Curse

"I swear it was Sir Reinhard!" Fable exclaimed, bouncing on her toes.

Nightwind had just dropped her and Timothy off in the yard of the old inn before retreating to his stable beside the house. No sooner had they gotten in the door than they had nearly tripped over Fedilmid. The old witch squatted on the ornate purple rug in the entryway of the Thistle Plum Inn, rummaging through a striped rainbow suitcase. An array of colourful socks lay scattered over the floor.

"My speaking stone, please, Fable." He held a hand towards her without even looking up from his task, which he continued one-handed.

"Oh." Fable took off the necklace and handed it to him.

"You're certain it was Sir Reinhard?" Fedilmid slung the stone around his neck and continued digging furiously through his bag without missing a beat.

"It was definitely him!" Timothy waved his hands

in the air as he spoke. He bumped the mahogany stand beside him and a vase of pink roses dotted with tiny white baby's breath flowers rocked precariously, threatening to empty its fragrant contents onto the floor. Fable caught the vase, steadying it, but Timothy hadn't even noticed.

They were surrounded by the luggage from Tulip Manor.

Fable spied hers, a purple duffle bag with blue polka dots. Her navy blue book bag, spangled with silver stars, lay draped across the top of it. She picked up the familiar wool bag and slung its strap over her shoulder. The weight of it was comforting, as if a missing piece of her had returned.

Fedilmid pushed aside some blue fabric in his suitcase that matched both his robe and Fable's bag. "Perhaps he's competing in the Battle of Prosperity."

"The Battle of Prosperity? Is that what the games are called?" Fable asked. "We saw the sign at the festival grounds."

Fedilmid picked a round jar just big enough to sit in his palm out of the suitcase and held it up to the light. He frowned. "Nose hair salve? Why would I bring this? I must be losing my mind in my old age."

Timothy nudged Fable with his elbow and gave her an impatient look.

Fable batted his bony arm away. "Er—Fedilmid?"

Fedilmid tossed the salve on the carpet. The jar rolled across the floor and disappeared beneath the flower stand. Fable followed the container and bent down to peer into the dark space. The salve had rolled all the way to the back against the baseboard. Beside it lay a crumpled piece of paper.

Behind her, Fedilmid continued, still sounding distracted by his quest. "Oh, right. Yes. The Battle of Prosperity. As you probably saw at the fairgrounds, it's a competition in all sorts of different sports. It's said that the winner brings prosperity and wealth to his city for the new season."

"How many cities are in Starfell?" Timothy asked. "I thought there were only two."

Fable lit a soft glow in her palm and illuminated the area beneath the flower stand. The glass jar glinted in the light. A familiar messy scrawl was now visible on the crinkled page.

Lying flat on the ground, she stretched her glowing hand as far back as she could, her shoulder jammed against the stand, and pulled the jar and the paper out one at a time.

After tossing Fedilmid the salve, she placed the page on the table and smoothed it out. Her pulse quickened as she examined what looked like a recipe written in black ink. There was a jagged tear at the top of the page. The letters -*ood* bled onto the page from the ragged edge. Fable's heart pounded in her chest.

It can't be. The missing page from her mother's journal!

On the floor, Fedilmid sat back on his haunches and glanced at the children. "It's usually a Mistford versus Stonebarrow type of thing, but some of the small outlying villages have competitors as well." He paused and rifled through the contents of his suitcase once more. "Since Sir Reinhard dresses up as a knight, it makes sense that he'd compete in something like this."

Timothy wrinkled his brow. "I'm pretty sure he's a legitimate knight. He has a sword and everything."

A feather from a pterippus's left wing, three scales from an uprooter's tail, a fang from the serpent who sleeps beneath the sea, the tongue of a toad-like man from the Deepwood Swamp . . .

Fable only knew of one toad-like man. *Arame!* The servant had helped the children escape Endora's mansion last summer. In doing so, he'd betrayed Endora, his mistress, and had to take his family into hiding for their protection.

Her hand shook as she stared at the page. It was a list of spell ingredients, all taken from magical beings. *But for what?* She scanned to the bottom of the page and her pulse froze.

Flame from a firehawk's last breath.

Star!

Star had been Fable's first friend in Starfell, guiding her through the Burntwood Forest. The squat, chicken-like bird had helped her find Fedilmid and save Brennus from having his hand cut off for thievery. Of course, there were lots of firehawks in the Burntwood, but Fable couldn't bear the thought of any of them dying for some magic spell.

Fedilmid chuckled, pulling Fable from her thoughts. She folded the list and stuffed it in her book bag. She would show it to her friends tonight. For now, she didn't want to worry the adults and cause Aunt Moira to be even more overprotective.

Fedilmid tossed a polka-dotted bow tie—which Fable was sure she'd never seen him wear—into the pile on the floor and continued his conversation with Timothy. "Knighthood is a profession of the past," he said. "How many armoured policemen do you see gallivanting around on shiny-plated horses? There are some who love to dress up, but it's all for show. Especially for the games." He paused. "It is very entertaining. We wouldn't want to miss it."

Fable's pulse thrummed in her ears. *How did the missing page get here?* It had to be recently. The paper wasn't dusty like the floor beneath the stand. *We've barely been in Mistford an hour, and I've already seen Sir Reinhard and found this list. What's next?* She picked at a loose thread on her sleeve, remembering how Sir Reinhard had smashed the glass of his portrait in Endora's library with a mighty heave of his sword. He seemed like a real knight to her.

But she couldn't forget the look he gave the kids when they saw him at the fairgrounds. He'd looked upset—angry even. *What if he isn't free? Maybe Endora has forced him to work for her now.* Fable would never forget the threats her great-grandmother made against Arame's family if he didn't use his portal magic for her. Could she have done the same to Sir Reinhard?

Timothy bounced around Fedilmid like he'd had some of Algar's caramel candy. "So, you'll take us to see him?"

"Him, and all the other competitors." Fedilmid glanced up at the kids. "I'm happy to hear he's safe. You must be so relieved—Aha!" He pulled a peach silk scarf from the suitcase and got to his feet. With a flick of his wrist, the scarf floated from his hand above their heads as if caught in a breeze. Fedilmid snapped his fingers and purple flowers blossomed over the fabric.

Fable gasped, and Timothy's mouth fell open.

"That's beautiful." Fable's voice was soft with

wonder.

Fedilmid's eyes gleamed as he plucked the scarf from the air. "It's a gift for Alice. I've enchanted it so she can change the colours at will." He flicked the scarf again, and a blue wave rippled over the blooms. They were now a vibrant turquoise colour.

"Here, Timothy. You try." Fedilmid handed Timothy the scarf.

Timothy snapped it in the air, and the flowers turned lime green. His face lit up. "Awesome!"

"Amazing. Learn that from Mike's Mystical Magic? I heard you wanted to go there to pick up some new tricks," Brennus teased in a droll voice.

Fable glanced in his direction. He stood at the bottom of the stairs with a fiery orange lizard the size of a teacup chihuahua on his shoulder.

"Piper!" Fable rushed forward and took the uprooter in her arms. He chattered as she scratched his portly belly. "Alice has been feeding you well."

"She sure has," Brennus said. "Come on, she's upstairs with Moira and Thorn. They sent me to haul up more bags."

"Where's Nestor?" Fable stroked Piper's head and the lizard closed his eyes.

"Where do you think?" Brennus darted his eyes to the ceiling.

"In his study, of course." Fedilmid took the scarf from Timothy and draped it over his shoulder. He piled his socks and other items into the suitcase and snapped it closed. "We'll help you bring these up to our rooms."

"Thanks." Brennus grabbed the handle of the nearest piece of luggage and started up the stairs, banging the case on every step in a series of *thunks*. Fedilmid hustled after him with the rainbow travel bag in his arms, followed by Timothy. Fable put Piper on her shoulder, picked up her luggage, and trailed after them

The Thistle Plum Inn was just as charming as she remembered. With its faded plum shutters, chipped pink siding, and towering columns, from the outside it looked like a cozy version of a haunted house—one with a grandmotherly ghost who would jump from the closet with a cup of tea and ask if your blankets were warm enough. The essence of Alice and Nestor lived in every nook and cranny. They'd lived here so long, it made sense, and the idea of someone else taking over someday made her sad. She couldn't imagine anybody else running this inn.

At the top of the staircase, an elderly lady with wispy waist-length grey hair greeted them. She held a wicker laundry basket piled high with fresh white sheets. "Fable, you've finally arrived."

"That she has." Fedilmid slid past her, transferred

the scarf from his shoulder to hers, and walked to a room a few doors down the hall. "I'll be out in a moment, just need to unload these bags."

Alice grabbed one end of the scarf and examined it. "Fedilmid, this is lovely! Thank you."

"I thought you might like it. Give it a flick, if you're so inclined." With a sideways grin, he disappeared inside the room.

"Excuse me, Alice." Brennus bobbed his head as he walked by. He glanced over his shoulder. "Timothy, you're staying with me."

Piper chattered in Fable's ear and dug his claws into her shoulder.

"Ouch! Okay, okay." Fable took him gently in her hand and placed him on the floor. As he scampered after Brennus, she noticed dull grey spots on his usually bright orange tail.

She turned to Alice. "What happened to his tail?"

"He's missing some scales." Alice shook her head. "Must have lost them slinking through the fence. Always sneaking around, the little monster," she said affectionately. "He'll heal up fine."

She set down the basket and pulled Fable into a hug. With her rosy pink cheeks, she looked just as spry as she did last fall. At eighty-five years old, it was a wonder she and her husband were still able to manage the ancient inn. Fable returned her squeeze and caught a whiff of lavender. She peered over the elderly witch's shoulder into the basket. Pocket-sized mesh bags filled with purple buds and brown knobby roots rested on top of the folded laundry.

Alice caught her gaze. "Lavender buds and burdock roots—to put under the pillows for sweet dreams." She stepped back and ruffled Fable's hair. "You must have grown three inches since I last saw you."

Fable flushed. "If only that were true. It's more like an inch and a half."

Alice laughed and turned to Timothy. She motioned for him to set down his bag. "And you must be Timothy. I've been waiting to meet you."

Timothy set down his suitcase and let her pull him into an embrace. "Nice to finally meet you."

Alice beamed at him. "Polite like your cousin, but I imagine you're just as wild when given the chance." She gave Fable a sideways look. "I won't forget the scare she and her friends gave us last year."

The door nearest to them burst open and Thorn stepped into the hallway. "Fable, Timothy. You're here!"

"They are." Alice stepped away from Timothy and picked up her laundry basket. "Get settled into your rooms, then come downstairs to help with dinner." She cast Thorn a knowing look. "We have a lot to discuss."

"Do we ever," Thorn agreed. "Fable, you're in here with me. Timothy, you're next door with Brennus."

"I know." Timothy picked up his bag. "See you downstairs in a few minutes?"

Fable nodded. "Of course." She followed Thorn into their room. It was almost the same as the room they stayed in last fall—perfectly pink and flowery. It held two twin four-poster beds and a nightstand with a vase of pink roses. The wallpaper had wildflowers sprawling across it like a meadow in the Windswept Mountains. Fable wondered what Timothy and Brennus's room looked like. She imagined Timothy's scrunched up face at the sight of the ladylike décor, and smirked. *There are probably no race cars or aliens.*

Thorn sat on the quilted covers of the bed nearest the window. Her suitcase lay open next to her. Fable shoved her baggage under the other bed and hung her book bag over one of the bedposts.

"What was with that look Alice gave you?"

Thorn frowned slightly and pulled the broken arrow from her vest. "Must be about my sister. Or, whoever it was. Nestor's description matches her perfectly, remember? Long red hair, tall, and skinny. And she carried a bow." She seemed calm while she said it, but there was a hint of longing in her voice. She turned to

Fable. "Do you think it's her?"

Fable sat on the quilted bed. "It *must* be her. Maybe we'll find her at that big tent at the festival grounds. That's where the games are. I bet the competitors practice in there."

Thorn spun the arrow in her fingers and cocked her head. "How do you know the big top is meant for the games?"

Fable leaned across the space between their beds. "Nightwind took Timothy and I to the fairgrounds this afternoon before we came here."

Thorn pointed the arrow at Fable, her eyes wide with excitement. "That's why you were late! Did you see anybody? Or any clues about Orchid?"

Fable nodded. "The sign for the games listed archery as one of the sports. I bet Orchid is competing in it."

A grin spread across Thorn's face and she tossed her copper mass of hair over her shoulder. She leaned her elbows on her knees. "She was always more competitive than me. Of course, she's also faster and a much better shot."

Fable reached forward and squeezed Thorn's hand. "I bet she's here. I'll talk to Aunt Moira and see if we can go first thing tomorrow."

"You don't think we can go tonight?"

"I don't think Aunt Moira would let us."

"Maybe I should talk to her."

Fable bit her lip. Nobody could understand her aunt the way she could, except maybe Timothy. She doubted Thorn would convince her aunt to let them out at night. "I'll talk to her and see if we can. Maybe she'll let us with an adult."

Thorn looked like she was about to say more, but instead she shrugged her shoulders. "I hope so. I know it's selfish, but I'm tired of being the only Folkvar around. I miss my home."

Fable wished she could ease her friend's heartache. As much as she wanted Thorn to feel like she belonged, the Folkvar girl did stand out in this city. Fable tried to remember what Thorn had said. *Like a soggy mushroom in a field of wheat? Or something.*

But what would happen after they found Orchid? The Folkvar girl might know where the remainder of Thorn's old colony had relocated. Would Thorn leave Tulip Manor? Fable swallowed and pushed the thought away. Reuniting the sisters would mean the world to her friend. No matter what, Fable was determined to do it.

"I have so much more to tell you," Fable said. "First, we saw Sir Reinhard at the festival grounds."

Thorn raised her eyebrows in surprise. "What? Are

you sure it was him?"

Fable nodded. "I'm sure of it. And so is Timothy. We must talk to him. He was hanging around the games tent. He looked angry for some reason." She frowned. "I hope Endora doesn't have him under some threat. Or a spell to control him."

"Maybe he's just worried about the games," Thorn said. "What else did you find out?"

Fable grabbed her book bag from the bed post and took out the wrinkled paper. She unfolded it and passed it to Thorn. "I found this in the entryway here. It's in my mother's handwriting."

Thorn's eyes grew round as tennis balls as she stared at the paper. "Is this—?"

"Yes." Fable nodded. "The missing page from my mother's journal. I'm sure of it." She pulled Faari's journal from the bag and opened it to the torn page. Thorn handed her the paper and Fable lined it up with the uneven tear.

It fit perfectly. *The Blood Curse* was written perfectly across the page in faded black ink.

She sucked in a breath. *I knew it.*

"How did it get here?" Thorn asked.

Fable got to her feet and smoothed her dress over her knees. "I don't know. But whoever took it must be staying here. Or must have stayed here recently."

"Do you really think it's somebody from Tulip Manor?"

Fable's throat thickened. "I hope not. It could have been torn away before my mother went there."

"That must be it," Thorn reasoned. "Why would anybody from Tulip Manor steal a spell list from you?"

Fable pressed her lips together. "I don't know."

A knock rapped against the door. Brennus's voice came from the hallway. "Are you two ready to come downstairs?"

"Yes," Thorn called back. She tucked the arrow away and stood. "We'll figure this out. Maybe Nestor can help."

"Maybe," Fable agreed. She got to her feet and grabbed her book bag from the bedpost. She slid her mother's journal next to the *Book of Chaos*. Whoever took the pages obviously didn't want her to know what was on them. But why would anybody want to keep a spell list from her? Was it somebody from Tulip Manor, or had the paper been there, beneath the table, for longer?

And what exactly is the Blood Curse? What does the spell do?

A loud clattering and a thump in the hallway interrupted her thoughts.

"What was that?" Fable righted her book bag

around her shoulder, rushed to the door, and pushed into the hallway with Thorn two steps behind her.

Brennus lay sprawled on the ground with Timothy at his side. A figure in a long, black cloak hovered over them, its back to Thorn and Fable. It raised its bony arms above its head.

Fable's heart leapt to her throat, sending panic coursing through her veins. Fable's magic took hold of that energy and drove it into her limbs. Green sparks crackled between her fingertips.

"Brennus!"

EIGHT

Tiny Skeletons

Terror clouded Fable's thoughts as the black-cloaked figure leaned over to examine its prey. *An undead!* She snapped her hands forward, but her magic twitched. Instead of her usual purple sparks, an emerald flame licked down her forearm. Alarmed, she flexed her fingers and tried to push down the fear.

What is happening to me?

The guard looked over its shoulder at the girls, and she faltered. A man with a long, hooked nose peered at her with bright green eyes, widened in surprise. It wasn't an undead at all. It was a man. A man who was very much alive.

Thorn placed her hands on Fable's shoulders and a warm cloak of peace eased over her. Fable's limbs relaxed, her friend's energy sedating her fear. The green flame receded into her skin like rain sinking into the ground.

"It's okay." Brennus let Timothy help him to his feet. "I was talking to Timothy, not watching where I was going. It was an accident."

Timothy pointed to the upturned cardboard box on the floor. A pestle and mortar lay at his feet amid several small bones, glass vials, and what looked to be the tanned hide of something small and furry. Fable grimaced. *Is that the skin of a rat?*

She lowered her hands and took a deep breath, forcing the white-hot energy to retreat from her fingers. "I'm—I'm sorry. Sir." Heat crept over her cheeks as she shook out her wrists, wringing out the magic like dishwater from a rag. "I thought—I didn't realize—" She gulped. *I'm such a bonehead.*

Timothy picked up the objects at his feet. The man turned the box right side up so the boy could place them back inside.

"I-it's all r-right, miss." He gazed at her in curiosity, much calmer now that the threat of a hurling mass of magical fire was gone. "No ha-harm done."

He was an odd-looking man, with a severe widow's peak and black hair even longer than Thorn's. Except, while the Folkvar girl's tresses were thick and bushy when not kept in a braid, his were thin and scraggly. It reminded Fable of a moss she'd seen on trees in the Lichwood—the type Thorn called *old man's beard.*

"I'm sorry for running in to you," Brennus said. "I didn't mean to. Honestly."

He and Timothy helped the strange man pick up the rest of his unusual objects and place them in the ragged box.

When they were done, Timothy thrust the package into the man's arms and wiped his hands. "I'm Timothy. And this is Brennus and Thorn." He jerked his head at the girls. "Fable, she's my cousin. She's the one who almost attacked you."

"I promise she's actually a nice person." Brennus cocked an eyebrow at Fable, a glint of mischief in his eyes.

Fable swallowed. *Am I really? I tried to blast this innocent man into next week.* Not that her magic obeyed. And what was that green flame? She shifted uneasily. *I've never done that before.*

The man held the box in front of his chest. He stared awkwardly at the floor. Murmuring his words, Fable could barely hear him when he said, "I'm Malcolm. Th-thanks for helping me pick up my th-things." He sent a quick glance at the children. "B-best be off to my room."

"Nice to meet you." Fable gave him a weak smile and rested her gaze on the box in his arms. *I wonder what he's got all those bones and weird trinkets for?*

Thorn pushed past Fable and met Brennus at the head of the stairs. "Too clumsy for your own good.

Can't even walk a straight line."

Brennus rolled his eyes and nudged her with his elbow. "Puh-leeze. I bet I can beat you down these stairs."

Thorn eyed him up and down, then bolted down the stairs.

"Hey!" Brennus bounded after her. "That's cheating!"

Fable turned to see Malcolm slink down the hallway and stop in front of the door at the very end.

"I'm sorry, again, sir," she called to him. Her face was warm, still tingling at the thought of the flames and what she almost did.

"It's f-fine, miss. R-really." Malcolm shifted the box to one arm and pulled a key from the pocket of his cloak.

Timothy waved at the man. "Hey, you forgot something."

Fable followed her cousin's gaze. A small skull lay near one of the plant stands along the wall a few feet from her cousin. With its long beak and wide eye sockets, it looked like it had once belonged to some type of bird.

Timothy pointed at it. "Right there. It's a weird, umm, bird's head. Thingy."

Malcolm balanced the box on his hip and left the

key stuck in the door. "Oh, ah, th-thank you." He looked at Timothy's hand to follow his pointing finger and blinked.

Fable followed his gaze. The skull was in her cousin's hand. She shook her head. She could have sworn that the trinket had been several feet from Timothy. How did he get it so fast?

Timothy strolled over to Malcolm and placed it in his box. The man was hugging it to his chest with white-knuckled fingers. He stared at Timothy.

Fable furrowed her brow. *Strange. It must have been closer than I thought. A trick of the light.*

Timothy gave the man an odd look. "Okay, well. I'm sure we'll see you around." He shrugged, then walked past Fable and started down the stairs.

Fable stared at the man. He avoided her gaze and pushed open the door to his room. With one last wide-eyed look at Fable, he slipped inside and shut the door.

Fable shook her head. She had to have been imagining things. Timothy didn't have magic. He never had. At their home in Rose Cottage, he tried so hard to do the spells Fable had attempted to teach him. But he'd never been able to even flicker a flame.

My brain must be rattled from my near miss. Fable frowned. Why did she think everything was an undead? She hated feeling like a scared rabbit stuck in a trap. Every unexpected movement sent her into a panic.

What was she going to do when Endora came after her again?

Fable's thoughts shot back to Squally Peak, when she was tied to Endora's chair with no way out. The woman's scarlet lips pulled back in a terrifying smile. *"I want the magic that's rightfully mine—the magic that runs through your veins."*

Fable shuddered, shaking the memory from her head. Gazing at her hands, she wondered where the flames had come from. They'd felt strange. Not hot, but not cold either. There had been no burning pain, just a whispered lick like a soft breeze against her skin.

She'd almost sent those flames hurling at an innocent man. Were they bad magic? Dark, like Endora? Something evil, growing from Endora's bloodline, within her?

Laughter floated up from the dining area. Fable pushed her thoughts to the back of her mind and started down the stairs.

As Fable entered the warm kitchen, her mouth watered at the delicious aroma of turkey soup. Alice greeted her by thrusting a stack of bowls into her hands. The elderly witch picked up a basket of silverware and headed towards the dining room. Thorn was right behind her, carrying a tower of fine china plates.

"Come dear, help Thorn and I set the table," Alice said over her shoulder. "I think the boys have the food under control."

Fable glanced at the butcher block island in the centre of the kitchen where Brennus stood slicing carrots and carefully placing them in a dish. Beside him, Timothy twisted open a jar of pickles. Bundles of green herbs, freshly picked, hung from the old window frame suspended from the ceiling above their heads. Behind them, Algar bent over a massive stew pot on the old wood-burning stove.

A dog bed in a wooden box labelled "Piper" sat beside the stove, making Fable smile. The uprooter had obviously found a loving home at the Thistle Plum, which was the best place for him until he could be returned to Brennus' mother.

"Coming, Dreamy Daisy?"

Alice stood by the door to the dining room looking at Fable expectantly. Fable nodded and gave the witch a sheepish smile. Where was her head today?

Fable followed Alice and Thorn, gripping the

bowls. They were so delicate they looked as though they would shatter at the slightest squeeze from her fingers, but her death grip proved that wasn't true. *Stars in Starfell*, she needed to relax. To take her mind off what she'd almost done to poor Malcolm, she decided to see if Alice had any of the answers she and her friends were looking for.

"Alice, have you seen the Odd and Unusual shop since last fall?"

Alice glanced over her shoulder at Fable. "No. We've checked several times and asked around, but the shop hasn't been back. It's been a quiet winter. Perhaps it will be back during the festival—when there are lots of tourists to sell strange items to."

"I hope so. Brennus would love to see his parents."

Once they were in the dining room, Fable carefully set the stack of bowls on the plum-coloured linen that covered the long table. Alice set down her basket and began to count the forks.

"Thorn," she said, without glancing up, "please set one of those plates at each seat. Fable, the bowls go on top. Make sure the red roses line up at the top."

The girls nodded. Thorn began to set the plates, scrutinizing the flowered pattern to make sure it sat properly. Fable followed behind her, placing a bowl on each plate with a soft clink, careful to line up the roses and not to chip the china.

"Where are Fedilmid, Aunt Moira, and Nestor?" Fable asked Alice as she worked.

The wizened witch held a fork up to her nose for inspection. "They're in his study, discussing his research—" She pursed her lips. "Not rinsed properly. Soap spots all over it." With a murmur and a light flick of her wrist, the fork glinted in the light. "Much better." She set the fork on the table to the left of one of the place settings, making sure it was perfectly straight before she picked up another one.

Fable's arm tensed as she set down another bowl. *Aunt Moira said I could talk to Nestor with her!*

Thorn stopped, balancing the remaining plates in one hand, and stared at Alice. "What kind of research?"

Alice's smile wavered, deepening the lines around her mouth. She waved a wrinkled hand in front of her. "Oh, you know. Astronomy. Divination is more my thing." She frowned. "Well, to be honest, my scrying isn't what it used to be. In fact, I've been having a lot of issues with it lately. But at least I have dear Nestor. He finds something new written in the stars every day."

"Like what?" Fable asked.

Alice drummed her fingers on the side of the basket. "Aunt Moira wants to tell you herself." She met Fable's gaze with her milky blue eyes. "I'm sorry. I wish I could tell you more."

Fable set down her bowls on the table. "Is it about the Blood Star? Please, Alice. I deserve to know. How can I be prepared for what Endora does next if I don't even know what the star is capable of?"

Alice bit her lip, then glanced at the doorway that lead to the hall. She sighed, "Yes, it's about that star Endora stole from you."

Fable's heart thudded against her ribs. "Is there a way to get it back?"

Sadness washed over her as she thought of the star slipping away from her and into Endora's soot-blackened fingers. Her great-grandmother may not have been able to perform the spell to steal Fable's magic, but Fable was sure she'd manage to use the star's power for something wicked. Her heart ached at the thought of the warm glow of the pretty rock in her hand. Fable had felt a connection between herself and the star, she was sure of it, like it *wanted* her to take it. But if that were true, why had it gone so easily to Endora's call?

She clenched her fists. *It was meant for me.*

Alice clucked her tongue and ran her fingers over the pink cloth that lined the basket's edge. She shuffled around the table until she stood beside the girls. She glanced over her shoulder, then leaned in and whispered, "Rumour has it, there's another spell Endora might use to unlock the star's potential."

Fable's chest tightened. "What do you mean, another spell?"

Alice leaned in further, her voice hushed. "Nestor found an old grimoire in the attic that mentioned star spells—"

"Alice Serpins." Aunt Moira's voice cut through the air like an oar slicing through the calm sea. "I told you I don't want the children to know about this. Not yet!"

Alice's cheeks turned bright red and she whirled around. Aunt Moira stood in the entry of the dining room, her arms crossed and a scowl on her face.

"Moira, she has a right to know." Alice folded her hands in front of her. "She's thirteen years old—"

"You've found nothing substantial." Aunt Moira's expression stiffened. "It's all just a hunch. Nestor hasn't been able to prove anything."

"Yet," Alice replied gently.

Fable slammed her stack of bowls on the table. "You were hiding this from me?" It was more of an accusation than a question.

Aunt Moira let out an exasperated sigh. "I just wanted to wait until we had something solid. You children go off on these wild goose chases—"

"And we haven't been wrong yet." Fable glared at her aunt, her hands on her hips. *How could she hide this from me? We've proven that we're capable and strong!* "We've done more to fight Endora than you ever have."

Aunt Moira closed her eyes and took a deep breath. "That's enough, Fable."

Alice and Thorn stood in silence, glancing back and forth between Fable and Aunt Moira's now brick-red face. Thorn picked up the remainder of the cutlery and continued to set the table, staring intently at the place settings as she worked.

Bubbling anger filled Fable, and her aunt's stubborn righteousness coursing through the air only fueled the fire of Fable's rage. Fable clenched her jaw and was about to say more when Brennus entered the room, balancing a platter of steaming rolls in his hands. He paused, taking in the scene around the table. A weak smile crossed his face.

"I'll come back in a few minutes."

Aunt Moira closed her eyes. "Brennus, wait. It's fine. We will discuss this later, Fable. At a more appropriate time." She plastered a fake smile on her face and waved her hand at the boy. "Set those on the table, please."

Brennus gulped and looked around the room as if he were looking for a way out of a firestorm. He glanced at Moira, who waved her hand at the table, then did as he was told and set the rolls in the middle of it.

A family Fable had never seen before entered the dining room. She lowered her fiery gaze. *They must be guests at the inn.*

The woman, clutching a small child's hand, flashed them a tentative smile.

"Is it almost dinnertime?"

Alice folded her hands in a warm gesture. "Any minute now. Please, take your seats." She cast Aunt Moira and Fable a stern look, as if to say *no drama in front of the guests!* "I'll check on the food."

Aunt Moira tilted her head as Alice left the room but kept the phoney smile. "Girls, the table looks lovely. Please, let's take our seats." She turned to the lady. "What a beautiful dress! Where did you get it?"

The woman flushed as the family took their places around the table. "Why, thank you! I made it myself."

Thorn heaved a sigh of relief, pulled back the chair

in front of her, and plunked down.

Fable swallowed her anger, letting it simmer in the pit of her stomach. She finished setting the bowls, then plopped down in the chair next to Thorn without saying a word.

Aunt Moira chatted amiably with the couple as if nothing were wrong. As if she hadn't just been in a heated discussion with her niece and the woman who owned the inn.

Fable leaned over and whispered in Thorn's ear. "We're going to get to the bottom of this. If there's a way that Endora can unlock the star's powers, we're in big trouble."

Thorn nodded and whispered back, "And so is all of Starfell." She glanced at Fable's wrists. "What happened upstairs earlier? How did you conjure those flames?"

Fable tucked her forearms beneath the table, worried they would appear again. She swallowed. "Just a trick Fedilmid taught me."

Thorn gave her a sideways look. "Weird trick." She picked up a roll from the tray on the table, split it open, and began to butter it.

Fable swallowed. What was she supposed to say? *It might be a sinister genetic defect I inherited from*

105

my evil great-grandmother? She could almost hear the lich's mocking laughter.

For a second, she thought about asking Aunt Moira about the flames. But right now, after their argument about the Blood Star, her aunt was the last person she felt like talking to. Besides, they were related by marriage, not by blood. Aunt Moira probably had no idea how Fable's magic worked. She could ask Fedilmid, who seemed to know a lot about all types of magic. But what were the chances that he would tell Aunt Moira?

No. This is something I need to figure out myself.

NINE

Whispers Behind Closed Doors

Fable crouched outside the mahogany door of Nestor's study. She glanced up and down the hall to see if anybody approached. Brennus squatted next to her, his ear pressed up against the door. Thorn knelt behind them.

After dinner, the adults had retreated upstairs and left the kids to clean up. The three of them had rushed through washing dishes and crept up to the office to see if they could find out what was going on. Timothy was the only the one to stay behind. He told Fable he had a headache, then went upstairs to bed.

Now, Brennus leaned in tighter to the door. "I can't understand them. It's all muffled."

"Let me try," Thorn whispered.

"Just a second." Fable placed her ear next to Brennus's, straining to hear what was being said inside the room. The five adults of Tulip Manor and the Thistle Plum were all in there. She couldn't make out what the hushed voices were saying, but they sounded urgent.

They must be talking about something important. Why can't they just tell us?

"Let me try. I have an idea," Thorn said.

Brennus poked Fable in the ribs. "Don't you have a spell for spying? Or enhanced hearing? Or to make us really tiny so we could sneak inside?"

Fable squirmed sideways and batted his hand. "My magic doesn't work like that." She wrinkled her nose. *To make us really tiny?* "I don't think anybody's does."

Thorn huffed. "I said, I have an idea."

She got to her feet and crept to the table that sat along the nearest wall, doing her best to muffle her footsteps. On the table sat two glass vases filled with dried pussy willows and wildflowers, limp and crumbling with age. She emptied the contents of one into a neat pile, then returned to her friends.

"Here. If you're not going to let me listen, you can use it." She handed the container to Fable.

Fable stared at the vase, trying to understand exactly what Thorn was getting at.

"Put its top against the door, then your ear up to the bottom," she instructed in a low voice. "It's a trick Orchid taught me. We used it to listen in on our parents when we'd done something bad. Helped to know what to expect when they were ready to dish out our punishment."

"I can't believe you'd do that. Spying on your parents." Brennus shook his head with a half-grin.

Thorn gave him a sideways look. "Orchid told me to. Besides, listening in was good for other things too. How else were we supposed to find out when the spring faeries were going to visit the garden?"

Brennus stared at her, looking like he was about to say something. But he gave his head a quick shake, closed his mouth, and then got to his feet and padded to the table. Seconds later, he returned with the other vase in his hand and knelt beside Fable again.

Fable pressed the top of the vase against the door and placed her ear on the bottom of it. Nestor's voice came through the glass, still dampened, but clear enough to understand.

"Trueforce said nothing was amiss at Endora's mansion. In fact, he seemed to think their sorcerer's spells had weakened her." Fable imagined the old man twisting his tweed hat in his hands. "He said she looked like a battered old crone, that she was back to living a natural life. Thanks to the Ministry's work."

Algar let out a grumble. "You mean, thanks to the kids."

"Of course, *we* know that." Fedilmid sounded distinctly annoyed. "Sergeant Trueforce, that old bellyacher. He'd love to take credit for it." He let out a flustered sigh. "He should know better."

"It's wishful thinking," Algar agreed. "He doesn't want to face the truth."

"What about what happened at Squally Peak?" Aunt Moira cut in. "What did he have to say about that?"

"He didn't seem to have much interest in it," Alice's soft voice replied. "Said he'd have his secretary set up a meeting to discuss it. She never did call us."

"Fable and I will pay him a visit. He can't keep shutting us out."

It was silent for a moment. Fable glared at the door, heat whirling in her chest. Sergeant Trueforce. The same hound-eyed policeman who'd dismissed Fable and Fedilmid last fall when they reported Endora's earlier activities.

Seems he hasn't changed his tune. Fable's stomach clenched at the memory of him holding the door open for them to leave, slopping coffee over his crumb-covered shirt.

Nestor's voice echoed in Fable's ear through the vase. "You can try. But his receptionist turned us away when we tried to see him last month. And he won't return our calls."

"Have you sent a letter with this information about the Blood Curse?" Fedilmid asked.

Fable and Brennus exchanged a glance.

Thorn leaned in closer to them. "What are they saying?"

"Ssh!" Brennus waved her back.

Thorn wrinkled her nose at him. She sat back on her heels.

Nestor chuckled. "Do you think they'd believe me? They already think I'm a crazy old man. If I told them I'd been scouring through ancient astronomy articles for information about a star that's already fallen, and that I've found another way to unlock its magic, they'd send me to the hospital to have my head examined."

Fable's stomach lurched. *New spell? The Blood Curse!* She pressed her ear harder into the glass.

"He has a point," Algar said. "I'm not sure we can trust Trueforce. Not right now."

"What is this new spell?" Aunt Moira's sharp voice interjected. "I thought we were safe after Fable's birthday."

Nestor cleared his throat. "I found it in an old copy of the *Magic and Lore of Starfell* from almost two centuries ago. Shortly after the Blood Star was created."

The Magic and Lore of Starfell? Fable remembered the giant tome on Endora's desk in her library, scribbling away about Fable as she approached it. In fact, it had even warned her that Endora had entered the room.

Fable saw it in the old crone's tent up on Squally Peak last fall. She was sure the woman still had it.

"I thought Endora stole the book." Aunt Moira's voice was sharp.

"She did," Nestor replied. "She has the original magical version that writes the history of Starfell as it happens. But copies have been made over the years of the old stuff. Heck, you can buy simplified versions of them at several of the stores here in Mistford."

"I've seen them at Madam Mildred's," Fedilmid agreed.

Nestor continued. "As we know, the star only responds naturally to those with good intentions. This curse is another way for somebody with, well, less than good intentions to unlock the star's magic. Endora's connection to the star will make it easier for her, but she'll still need something—er—physical from somebody magical of her bloodline, since she's so, well, you know, *different*—"

Endora's connection to the star? What does he mean by that?

Aunt Moira's voice grew higher. "Like what?"

"Well, it could be anything. A strand of hair, a fingernail clipping, even a flake of skin would do."

Relief flooded Aunt Moira's voice. "So, it doesn't have to be blood."

Alice spoke up. "No, it doesn't have to be blood." She paused. "Although somebody with Endora's mind-set may think blood would be strongest."

Nestor continued, "The other ingredients are rare, and quite barbaric really. For example," he paused and there was a rustle of papers, "a *flame from a firehawk's last breath.*"

Star. Fable thought of her plucky chicken-like friend and guide through the Burntwood forest when she first fell through the *Book of Chaos*. Her heart twinged. *That was on the list from my mother's journal!*

"And this—" Fable could hear the frown in Nestor's voice. "The—erm—*tongue of a toad-like man from the Deepwood Swamp.*"

Fable's hand shook so hard she almost dropped the vase. Again, exactly like the list in her book bag. She remembered Arame's bulbous eyes as he grasped her hand before transporting her home from Endora's library. And the tongue he'd licked his eyeball with to do it. He looked more like a toad than toads did.

Brennus squeezed her leg with his free hand. His eyes reflected the frozen terror in her heart.

"Can I see that?" Aunt Moira asked.

Several footsteps and a shuffling noise sounded from inside the room. After a pause, Aunt Moira spoke again. "*A fang from the serpent who sleeps beneath the sea*—this is rubbish. Moranda is a myth."

Moranda? Who's Moranda?

"Well, actually, she was quite real," Nestor stammered.

"She died hundreds of years ago," Algar added.

"Endora could go after the body," Fedilmid said.

The study fell quiet.

Thorn prodded Brennus's shoulder. "What's going on? Why do you two look like a forest ogre has sprouted in there?"

"Ssh!" Brennus hissed at her. "We'll tell you in a minute."

Finally, Aunt Moira broke the silence in the room. "We need to keep the children in sight at all times."

"Moira—" Fedilmid said gently.

Aunt Moira wasn't having it. "I'm serious, Fedilmid. Endora is after Fable, and she doesn't care who she hurts along the way. As long as she gets what she wants."

"I know—"

"No, *I* know," Aunt Moira interrupted. "Let's not forget this awful woman murdered her own grandchildren! Her great-granddaughter is nothing to her. And neither are the rest of us."

Fable nearly choked. Suddenly, every fear and dark

114

emotion in the study hit her like a freight train at full throttle, sending a green spark through her fingers. The vase clattered to the floor.

Brennus cast her a concerned look. He took a deep breath, then grabbed her hands. His friendship and warmth coursed over her. Thorn quickly placed her hands on Fable's shoulders and let her own healing and love mingle in with Brennus's. Fable's magic calmed, but her heart still burned.

Fable had known that Endora had killed her parents and uncle. But she had thought it was in a rockslide set off by the woman's chaotic magic. She hadn't known it was on purpose—that it was murder.

Fable squeezed her eyes shut and gripped Brennus's hands. Was that depth of evil growing inside her, planted from the great-grandmother she barely knew? Was that why Endora wanted Fable's power so badly? It would explain the flames and why Fable couldn't control her magic. Why despite her good intentions, she hurt Grimm—the dog she loved more than anything.

Fable had the sudden urge to run away from the inn and everybody in it.

Footsteps sounded from within the room, getting louder as they approached the door. Brennus sprang to his feet and pulled Fable with him. "Let's go!"

Thorn grabbed the vases and placed them haphazardly on the table and the trio set off down the stairwell before anybody could see them. Only a few steps down, Fable heard the door creak open and paused to listen. Somebody was looking down the hallway.

Thorn, in the lead, kept going.

Endora murdered my parents. Her own family! Fable sucked in a breath and flexed her fingers. The lich's hunched form and soot-blackened face grinned maniacally in her head. *And how much worse am I going to get? Am I going to become just like her?*

Brennus tugged at Fable's hand. "Come on."

Fable relented and followed her friends down the darkened stairway.

Woodsy Tea

Fable sat with her feet tucked up on the armchair in the corner of her and Thorn's room. Her mother's journal lay on her lap, open to the spell list. She gazed out the barred window at the half-moon, shining above the thatched roof of Nightwind's stable. She wondered if Nightwind was inside his cozy stall, either sleeping or enjoying the soft mash she saw Nestor take out to him earlier.

The first time she'd seen the pterippus, he had stood hobbled beside Endora's canvas tent on Squally Peak, his head and wings drooping to the ground. Later, Fable had been trapped inside that tent with the evil woman. The lich had said Fable's blood was the key ingredient for the nasty spell to gain control of Fable's magic—but it had to be done that night. The night the Blood Star fell.

Part of Fable hadn't believed Endora would really do it. She'd seen the hesitation in her great-grandmother's eyes. But the heinous woman had proven Fable wrong. She had pulled a dagger from her pocket and held it to Fable's throat. *If Brennus hadn't gotten there in time*—Fable shook her head. No, she couldn't think that way.

But she needed to stop underestimating what Endora was capable of. The lich had used her picture frames to suck the lives of dozens of people dry to maintain her youth and beauty. She'd even tried to do that to Timothy. And she'd been willing to kill Fable to increase her own power—almost succeeding more than once. And, apparently, she'd already murdered Fable's parents and uncle. To a woman like that, killing a firehawk and an ex-underling would mean nothing. It would be easy.

The door to the room swung open and Thorn entered, carrying two steaming cups of tea. The smell of peppermint mixed with something earthy and comforting filled the room. Brennus followed behind her with a mug in his hand and shut the door.

"Where's Timothy?" Fable asked.

Brennus took a seat on Thorn's bed, cradling the ceramic mug in his hands. "He's got a headache. Alice is brewing a potion to help him. Something that looks like chamomile but smells like dirt."

"Feverfew." Thorn set one of the teacups she carried onto the doily covered nightstand beside Fable.

Tea sloshed over the rim onto the lace. "It's good for headaches. My mom used to use it when Orchid and I were too rowdy."

Brennus wrinkled his nose. "Whatever it is, I hope she adds chocolate to mask the flavour. There's no way that something that smells like a dead frog is going to taste good."

"How do you know what a dead frog smells like?" Thorn plunked down beside him on the bed.

Brennus lifted his mug to avoid spilling. "Hey!"

Thorn smirked, not looking very sorry.

The gangly teen steadied his tea with both hands and gave the Folkvar girl an annoyed look. "How *don't* you know what a dead frog smells like?"

Thorn rolled her eyes, then flicked her gaze to Fable. "How are you feeling?"

Fable picked up her tea and wrapped her hands around the warm cup. "Okay, I guess. I mean, it's pretty weird hearing all that stuff about Endora and my parents." She bit her tongue. The name left the same taste in her mouth that she imagined Alice's concoction would leave in Timothy's.

Brennus nodded. "And now she's after Star and Arame too." He paused. "And Moranda."

"Who's Moranda?" Fable asked. "Aunt Moira didn't believe in her."

Thorn's face drew tight. "Moranda? She's a sea serpent. Or was a sea serpent. A long time ago."

Brennus thrummed his fingers on the handle of his mug. "Like Algar said, she's been dead for hundreds of years."

"Slayed by the very fisherman that were her prey," Thorn added. "It's said her body lies at the bottom of the Bottomless Sea, south of the Burning Sands."

"How can anything lay at the bottom of a bottom-less sea?" Fable asked.

Thorn shrugged. "That's just what people say."

"From what I've read in Fedilmid's books, it's not actually bottomless," Brennus said. "It's just really deep."

"Maybe we could use the guitar to see if Moranda is really there." Thorn glanced at Brennus. "If we got it right, we could find Star. And Orchid too!"

Brennus lowered his eyes. His fingers tightened around his mug. "I haven't been able to make it work at all. Yet. But I will. I have to."

Thorn's expression softened. "Maybe Nestor has a book that would help."

Brennus shrugged. "Maybe," he said, but he didn't sound hopeful.

"Hey." Thorn thumped his knee affectionately with her fist. "You'll get it."

He gave her a half-smile. "Thanks."

Fable glanced at the crumpled sheet she'd tucked into Faari's journal. She had smoothed the spell list out as best she could and placed it along the edge it had been ripped from.

"All those weird spell ingredients are here on that page from my mom's notebook." Her stomach tensed. "And now Endora is searching all over Starfell for them. We have to stop her. There's just so much to do. We must find Orchid, figure out Endora's plan, go to the Burntwood forest to warn Star, somehow figure out where Arame is hiding . . ." She paused, her heart hammering in her chest. She shot a glance at Brennus. "Of course, there's still your parents and the situation with Ralazar—"

Thorn held up her free hand. "You're not responsible for all this. We need to take it one step at a time."

Brennus had a pained look on his face, as if he were struggling to find the right words. "I want to find my parents again more than anything. But they aren't going anywhere—well, anywhere outside their shop that is. I need more time to research anyways. We'll figure it out."

"Plus," added Thorn, "you said Sir Reinhard is at the festival. I bet he can help us."

Fable took a deep breath. Her friends were right.

Isn't that something Fedilmid had taught her? One step at a time. No matter how small, each step in the right direction will get you closer.

She transferred her teacup to her other hand, closed the book, and set it on the nightstand. "With Aunt Moira hovering over us, how are we going to get to the bottom of this? We'll be lucky if she lets us even go to the festival, let alone speak to Sir Reinhard now. And she'll never let us search for Star and Arame—or any of their kinds—to warn them. We're not even supposed to know about the spell."

Brennus tapped his slim fingers on his mug. "Fedilmid might talk some sense into her."

Thorn raised a brow. "After what we pulled last fall when we promised to stay in the yard? And ended up in a completely different town?"

Brennus's grin faded. "We'll get away from the adults if we have to. And maybe we can find that grimoire in Nestor's study. I've been meaning to ask him if he has any books about warlock curses."

Thorn raised her brows. "You think he'd just let us read that grimoire with the spell?"

"We can sneak in there if we have to."

Guilt crept up Fable's spine at the thought of sneaking behind Aunt Moira's back. Her aunt had always been overprotective. After learning about the new spell, Fable was sure she would watch the teens' every move.

Brennus blew gently on his tea, then took a sip. He sputtered and coughed, then held the mug away from his face with a twisted scowl.

"Ergh! What is this?"

Thorn shot him a look of disdain. "I mixed some of Alice's valerian root with the peppermint leaves. I thought we'd need some help to settle down." She paused and took a sip, then smacked her lips. "It's a bit woodsy. But it's not as bad as feverfew."

"Woodsy?" Brennus spat the word. "It tastes like dirt. And bark. And old spongey moss!"

Thorn took another sip from her cup, then gave Brennus a sideways glance. "Exactly. Just like the forest."

Fable placed her tea on the nightstand. Despite Thorn's good intentions, she wasn't sure which was better—struggling to sleep or drinking this dirt-flavoured potion.

It can't be as bad as the spell Endora is brewing. The thought of that woman searching for new ingredients sent a shiver through Fable. *If she's capable of murdering her own family, then what kind of horrible things am I capable of?* The terrifying picture of Grimm, unconscious on the ground, broke through her thoughts. *And how am I going to stop her if I can't even stop myself?*

Chimes tinkled through the dimly lit shop. Clarice glanced up from the worn ledger she'd been filling with that day's sales. The backwards letters painted on the storefront window that spelled *Madam Mildred's* gleamed in the light from the lamppost outside.

A man stood in the doorway. Something bone-thin and not-quite-human wearing a flowing black cloak towered behind him.

The man looked like he'd tumbled into a pig pen and wrestled a hog. His greasy dark hair hung in clumps around his shoulders, and his wiry frame bent at odd angles as if he'd spent the night sleeping in a box.

A coffin, maybe. Clarice shook her head. No, she knew better. It was just Doug.

Must be back for more information for that haggard old lich. She scrunched up her face in distaste and lay down her pencil. *I don't have anything for him. I haven't seen hide nor hair of that child since last fall. Or the old fool of a witch either.*

"We're closed." Clarice stuffed the ledger in the drawer beneath the cash register. "Can't you read?"

Doug ignored her and entered the shop. He side-stepped a display that teetered with vials, tubes, and bottles. The cloaked figure followed him, gliding eerily over the floor. The cloak's hood draped over its head, hiding what Clarice knew would be a skeletal, disfigured face.

"Door's open. Yeh'd be wise to lock it if yeh was closed."

Smart aleck. Clarice slammed the drawer shut and cast the undead creature a wary glance. She strode to the front of the store, her dull grey skirt swishing with her angry steps.

"What do you want, Doug?" She placed a spindly hand on her bony hip.

"Nice to see yeh again, too," he said with a wave of his hand. "Always such a pleasure."

Clarice pursed her lips. "Get on with it."

Doug jerked his head at the undead, who stood stoically behind him. "First off, I need a glamour potion for me mate."

"A glamour potion?" Clarice gawked at the guard. "Are you trying to make him easier on your eyes?"

Doug glared back at her, which deepened his frown lines further. "'Ow else is 'e s'posed to slip by unnoticed at the festival? I need to make 'im look as—er—alive as poss'ble."

125

"Why are you taking him to the festival? Of all the things—"

"None o' yer business."

Clarice narrowed her eyes at the filthy henchman. "Go on."

He pulled a crumpled paper with torn edges from the front pocket of his stained shirt and unfolded it. With an annoyed look in her direction, he cleared his throat. "White yarrow harvested on a gibbous moon, burdock root grown beneath a hawthorn bush, flame from a firehawk's last breath—"

"Stop!" Clarice narrowed her eyes at the man. "We don't carry *those* kinds of ingredients here. We're a children's shop! Vanity spells, tricks, and little enchantments, sure. But those things on your list are for serious magic. You'll have to visit the Arcane Scroll." She paused. "But I doubt even they will have some of those nasty components. You might want to try the spring festival for the firehawk. I hear the Magical Menagerie is town. You know—the petting zoo with magical creatures."

A greedy smile crossed Doug's lips. "Magical creatures, eh?"

"What are you up to?"

The henchman sniffed, then wiped his nose with the back of his hand. He folded the paper and shoved it in his pocket. "Again, none o' yer business. These is for Endora."

"I thought she was trapped in that mansion of hers." Clarice replied. *Where she belongs.* The old wretch had once promised to share her secret to youth and beauty with Clarice in exchange for information. Clarice had yet to see any type of payment. *Ungrateful hag.*

Doug snorted. "Yeh think a woman o' her power is jest gonna be toiling away there waiting to die?" His face darkened. "She has plans, yeh know. She's gonna get out and she's gonna get that little brat back. And get the power she deserves." He paused, his eyes glinting greedily in the light. "And pay me enough to live as a free man, o' course. No more diggin' graves for Doug." He glanced at the undead, still standing passively with its skeletal hands folded together. "No offense."

It didn't respond.

Clarice shuddered. *Foul creature.* It wasn't natural, all these dead bodies wandering around Starfell. *And twice now inside my place of employment!*

The creature's head turned in her direction. Its hood slid down to reveal the lifeless, black sockets where its eyes should be.

She recoiled from its gaze. *It's as though it's reading my mind.*

"Here's your vanity potion." Clarice grabbed a

glamour potion from the shelf behind her and thrust it into Doug's hands. "You need to leave. That thing—" she pointed a crooked finger at the undead "—gives me heebie-jeebies. It's bad enough that necromancer is in town spreading his filth. Probably raising bodies all over the place."

"Necromancer, yeh say?"

Clarice wrinkled her nose. "Yes. I forget his name. The one from Stonebarrow with a nose like a bird's beak. Strange man. But of course he is. Nobody normal has bone magic."

Doug stroked his chin and looked thoughtfully at the undead. "Hmm. I'm sure Endora will be interested to 'ear this bit of info, eh, big guy?" He nudged the creature with his elbow.

The undead stared at him blankly.

"Eh, liven up." Doug swung open the door and held it wide. "Yer goin' ter 'ave to act somewhat alive ter 'ang around the festival unnoticed."

The figure picked up the hem of its robes with its skeletal hands and danced a very jagged, crooked, bone-creaking jig. Once it stopped, it stared at Doug as if for affirmation.

Clarice grimaced. *Sure, it'll fit in perfectly among the living.* How could Endora stoop to using such disgusting servants?

Doug furrowed his brow and swatted the air. "Not like that. Yeh'll scare ev'ry livin' thing within a mile. Even the blasted crows will be flappin' away from yeh."

The creature shrugged, then glided out of the shop.

"Goodnight, Clarice," Doug said over his shoulder as the door chimed above him. "A pleasure, as always."

Clarice slammed the door behind him and bolted the locks.

Foul man up to no good for an equally foul old crone. She hoped that was the last time she'd see the loathsome henchman stroll into this shop.

Unless it was to reveal Endora's secret. She thought about that for a moment. "Pah!" she said and waved her hand dismissively. She wasn't even sure eternal youth would be worth the price. She'd grown used to being an ornery old shrew. Deep down, she was starting to like it.

Waving away the last of Doug's foul odour, she turned on her sensible heel and went back to her books.

The Arcane Scroll

"I knew that was going to happen." Fable followed her aunt from the Ministry's reception area into the sunshine outside. A warm breeze swept a wayward tress of black hair across her face. She pushed it aside and squinted at the blazing clock, shining like the midday sun above them. "It was just like Alice said. He doesn't want to believe us—or even hear what we have to say."

Aunt Moira gave a haughty huff and straightened her skirt, her bangles jangling in furious agreement. "We'll come back with Fedilmid and Algar. Thorn and Brennus too, if we must. Trueforce can't ignore us forever."

This visit had gone even worse than the last one. At least then the sergeant had spoken to her. Today, his assistant had insisted Trueforce was in meetings all morning. *Monumental meetings about substantial things*, she'd said.

More like napping on a pile of unfinished paper-

work. Fable swallowed a snort, remembering his disastrous office the last time she'd visited. His desk had been covered with stacks of loose papers, dirty coffee rings, and layers of crumbs. It had seemed to Fable that he would rather eat cookies all day than actually do his job.

Aunt Moira adjusted a pin in her bun, then marched down the stone steps to the sidewalk below. Fable pushed the strap of her book bag higher onto her shoulder and hustled after her aunt.

Moira's elbows jutted out like pointy weapons as she strode down the street. It reminded Fable of when her aunt would march across the yard at Rose Cottage to scold Grimm for digging up the marigolds. Or Timothy for climbing the spruce tree on the other side of the fence after his football. Or Fable for somehow "throwing" it into the needled branches.

Fable smiled to herself. As much as she had felt trapped and stifled in the mundane town of Larkmoor, her home at Rose Cottage still held memories that were close to her heart. It was where she'd spent the most formative years of her life, growing up with Timothy under Aunt Moira's watchful eye. There was no tolerance for witchcraft or sorcery in Larkmoor, but they'd made a different kind of magic there. And it was a simpler, safer life than out here in Starfell—in the place where magic was certainly real. And as wonderful as that magic was, sometimes it could bite.

Now, Aunt Moira clenched and unclenched her jaw, as if trying to chew through her angry thoughts. Fable kept pace a few strides behind, giving her aunt some space.

A few minutes later, they arrived at a black brick storefront with golden-edged windows. A matching black-and-gold sign covered with glittering stars hung above the door. The metallic letters scrawled across it read "The Arcane Scroll".

Excitement coursed through Fable. She'd been dying to visit the magic store since their last trip to Mistford, but the impromptu shift of Ralazar's shop to Firdale—with Fable and her friends inside it—had gotten in the way.

Aunt Moira's scowl slipped from her face. She glanced at Fable with a delighted gleam in her eye. "The Arcane Scroll. Your uncle and I used to come here often. I wonder if they still sell runes?" She paused, a wistful look on her face. "Oh, Fable. You're going to love it."

She traipsed up the steps and held open the door for her niece, the chimes tinkling merrily above them. Inside, the scent of cloves and honey met Fable's nose. Twinkling lights hung above wood-panelled walls lined with shelves. Some were filled with baskets of herbs, some with books, and others held varying arrays of trinkets. Glistening gemstone orbs, beaded necklaces, candles, and gnarled wooden wands sat on display tables covered with black lace.

But the most amazing of all was the enchanted ceiling. It was splattered with stars in glittering constellations. Fable gaped at the galaxy above her, wondering if it mirrored what Nestor saw through his telescope every evening. Did it reflect the night sky of Starfell? Had the Blood Star shone up there before it fell?

"Isn't it lovely?" Aunt Moira bustled through to a display table filled with vibrant decks of cards. Her face lit up as she picked one up to examine its artwork.

The group from the Thistle Plum had already arrived and were browsing the shelves and displays. Timothy beckoned to Fable from a bookshelf along the side wall.

"Fable, check this out!" He tapped the bottom of the shelf. With a creaky groan, the books slid upward into the ceiling to reveal a display of tiny animal skeletons and bones that reminded Fable of Malcolm's collection. Timothy's eyes were wide with enchantment. He ran a finger over what looked to be the skull of a mouse. "Cool, huh?"

"Amazing," Fable breathed. Her magic hummed

inside her, as if sensing the power in this shop. But it was a happy hum. Her whole body felt at ease here, as if she belonged.

She heard Fedilmid's voice somewhere in the shop and, looking around, she spotted him at the till. He spoke to a woman behind the counter wearing sunshine-yellow robes and layers of stone bead necklaces around her neck.

The clerk pushed her oversized glasses up her nose and shook her head. Her bouncy dark curls bobbed around her shoulders. "We're right out. It's too bad you weren't here an hour ago. We just sold the last ounce."

"No yarrow or wormwood either?" Fedilmid asked.

"I'm sorry, Fedilmid. Like I said, we just sold out of all our best spell-enhancing herbs." The woman shrugged helplessly. "Two strange men came in earlier with a big list of ingredients and bought them all. It was the strangest thing."

"What was strange about it?"

She tugged at one of her curls and frowned. "Well, they also asked for some bizarre components we would never carry here. Nasty things."

Strange men? Nasty things? Fable edged closer to the counter, leaving Timothy's side as he admired the leathery wing of a bat. She pretended to examine a display of ornate wooden boxes, her attention on the adults' conversation.

"Really?" Fedilmid stroked his pointy beard. "Strange men, you say?"

The lady wrinkled her nose. "Yes. The shorter one smelled horrible. Like he'd slept the night in a barn. And the tall one—" she hesitated, then pressed her lips together. "Well, I shouldn't speak badly of others. It isn't nice. We don't know what people are going through, do we?"

"That's very true." Fedilmid tugged at his pointed beard, glanced over his shoulder, and then leaned his elbows on the counter. "Not that it's any of my business, but do you remember what else was on their list?"

Fable's pulse quickened.

Somebody tapped on her shoulder from behind.

She startled, almost dropping the box in her hand. Shakily, she spun to see her friends. Brennus had a canvas bag slung over his shoulder and two books in his hands that couldn't have looked any more different. One had a sparkly purple cover and the other was bound with leather so worn that Fable thought it must have been a hundred years old.

Thorn stood beside him, eyeing the books with an eager look.

"I found a book on astral projection!" Brennus thrust the glittery book at Fable. "There are clear directions on how to do it right. I just need to buy these stones—"

Fable jerked her head towards Fedilmid and the clerk. "I'm trying to listen."

Brennus frowned but followed her gaze. "What're they talking about?"

At the till, Fedilmid drummed his fingers on the counter. "Well, that's too bad. Alice was hoping I could pick up some dried yarrow to strengthen her divination tea. She has mugwort and dandelion root, but it needs an extra boost. Do you have anything that might help?"

The clerk pulled a weathered notebook from a drawer beneath the till and opened it on the counter. She adjusted her glasses and skimmed the page. "Hmm. What about camphor? We have a bit of that left in the back. Let me grab some for you."

She slid from her stool and shuffled to the swinging door that must have led to the back room.

Drat! I missed what she said about the other ingredients.

Fable set the box on the table and turned her attention back to her friends. "Sorry. I thought they were talking about the Blood Curse."

Brennus tapped the spines of his books impatiently. "What did they say?"

"It sounds like some men were in here earlier and

bought all the divination herbs, including yarrow." Fable bit her lip. "It's on the list from my mother's journal."

Thorn shrugged. "Yarrow is a common part of most witch spells."

"I thought it could have been Doug, but she said it was two men. Unless he brought an undead—"

Brennus tapped his book against his hand, an incredulous look on his face. "You think he'd bring an undead in here? They'd call the police immediately. It would have blended in during the Parade of Expiration, but nobody wears costumes like that to the Spring Festival."

"Oh," Fable relented. *He must be right. There is no way Doug would get away with walking around with an undead in broad daylight. Not in this city.* "You two find some interesting books?"

Brennus held up the purple book and shook it in Fable's direction. "*Astral Projection for Fledgling Wizards.*" He flipped it open to the first chapter. "It says here we need strong magic. We have the guitar, but it might need a boost. According to this, holding a moonstone could stimulate the energy." He paused. "I don't have any money to buy a moonstone, but maybe Alice has one we could borrow. Do you think you could help? Your magic might do the trick. Maybe tonight we could try to astral project again."

Thorn's face lit up. "We can try to find Orchid. It might be easier than your parents, since she's close by." Her cheeks flushed. "If that Folkvar is her, I mean."

Brennus shot her a disgruntled look. "But the guitar is connected to my parents. Its magic transported them to Endora's wall. My mom's the one who figured out its magic."

Thorn pursed her lips but didn't respond.

"Yes, I'll help." Fable said. "Maybe it will work better now that we're in Mistford—the city Ralazar's store is attached to." She paused, remembering that her friends would have passed by the Odd and Unusual shop's magical tethering point on their way to the Arcane Scroll. "I'm guessing the shop wasn't there this morning?"

Brennus sighed and closed the book. "No. It must be in another town. If I could get the guitar to work, I could at least let my parents know we're in Mistford. Then my mom could try to direct the store here."

"She doesn't have the guitar to help her do that," Fable pointed out.

Brennus jutted his chin. "My mom's smart, and that shop is filled with weird stuff. If anybody's determined enough to find something magical in that junk heap, it's my mom."

Thorn nodded to the other book in Brennus's hand. "Tell her about this one."

"Oh, yeah. Speaking of the Blood Curse." Brennus looked at the counter where Fedilmid stood paying for his herbs, and then handed the book to Fable. "It's an old copy of the *Magic and Lore of Starfell*."

Fable's eyes widened and she took the book from her friend. "Where did you find this?"

"On the history shelf," Thorn replied. "Look at page one hundred and forty seven."

Brennus peered around Thorn's arm as Fable flipped to the page. The words *The Blood Star's Curse* were scrawled across the top with faded black ink. Her breath hitched.

"The Blood Curse."

Thorn nodded gravely. "The ingredients match up. Look at what it does to the star."

Fable turned back to the page. *Once the spell has been prepared, add the star to the cauldron on a new moon and let it simmer while the moon is waxing. On the next full moon, remove the Blood Star. Be warned, it will have lost its lustre. But rest assured, its bond to only serve good will be broken. Its power will be yours to do as you wish. It will bend to even the worst of intentions, enhancing your magic to cosmic levels. It can stop the aging process. It can make the most repul-*

sive person so charming that nobody can resist them. It can create chaos, havoc, but most importantly—power. Use with caution. If this curse is broken, the star will revert to its original state and seek to balance any negative effects it has caused.

Bend to even the worst of intentions? Create chaos and power? Fable's mouth went dry. If Endora knew about this spell, Fable was sure they were all doomed. She'd be able to use it to break her bonds to her mansion. Or to live forever. Or to gain power and control and wealth—and Fable already knew she wouldn't be afraid to hurt anybody in her path.

A loud gasp from behind Thorn interrupted Fable's thoughts. She looked around her friend to see a red-faced woman fumble with a book in her hands. She stared at Thorn, who was hunching to avoid hitting her head on the windchimes dangling from the ceiling, then down at the book, and thrust it back onto the shelf beside her.

"Er—excuse me." The lady ducked her head, then pushed by Fable and her friends. She glanced at them over her shoulder, then disappeared around a display of salt rocks and lamps.

That was rude. What's her problem?

Brennus followed her with his gaze, his brow furrowed. "What was that all about?"

140

Thorn pulled the book the woman had been reading from the shelf. The cover had a photo of lush pine trees and the title read *History of the Greenwood Forest*. The Folkvar girl flipped it open, ran her finger over the first page, then turned it to a spot about halfway through the book. Her frown deepened and her eyes flashed yellow.

"It says here that Folkvars are mysterious and fierce beings that lurk in the Greenwood. Due to their large size, they are dangerous and violent, often seen carrying weapons as big as a normal man." She slammed the book closed and shoved it back onto the shelf with a shaking hand. "That's not true! We're protectors of the forest, but violence is our last resort. We aren't aggressive."

"Yeah," Brennus added. "The only things quaking in their boots when you show up are mushrooms."

Fable shook her head in disbelief. She knew from Thorn that Folkvars were gentle guardians of the woods who loved yoga and didn't even eat meat. Sure, when she first met Thorn she'd been intimidated by her new friend's giant ax. But Thorn had only ever used it in defence. And now, the weapon was lost in Endora's mansion.

Thorn gritted her teeth, her hands clenched into fists. "This city—it's horrible. These people are so judgemental and have no idea about anything. I don't belong here."

Fable's heart lurched and she reached for her friend's arm. "You do. You're one of us. I know how you feel. In Larkmoor—"

Thorn jerked her arm away. "No, you don't. Sure, in Larkmoor you had to keep your magic a secret. But you didn't look different than everybody. Did people stare at you? Whisper when you walked by? Kick you out of their stores?"

The blood drained from Fable's face. She hadn't meant to upset her friend even more. She'd just wanted to help. "No, but—"

Thorn cut her off with a huff, then stomped past the display tables and out the door.

"Thorn!" Fable called after her.

Brennus gazed at the door with a troubled look on his face. "You go see if she's okay. I'll put the history book back and ask if Fedilmid will buy the astral projection one."

He held out his hand to Fable. She gave him the leather book and made her way outside. Thorn sat on the front steps of the store with her eyes closed and her hands gripping her knees. Quietly, Fable sat down next to her.

After a few deep breaths, Thorn opened her now mossy-green eyes. "We aren't dangerous or aggressive. We aren't monsters."

"I know." Fable looped her arm through the crook in Thorn's elbow. She didn't know what else to say. Her heart ached for her friend. It wasn't fair. If people could set their judgement aside and get to know Thorn, they'd see her for who she was. Somebody with a huge heart, a strong but gentle nature, and the best friend anybody could ask for.

And she's right. I shouldn't compare our situations.

"I'm sorry. I know it's different for you."

Thorn looked at her from the corner of her eye. "You don't have to fix this. Or try to make me feel accepted. I know I fit in at Tulip Manor. I know you're my family. But out here, in this city, it's different. I have to constantly be on guard or try to blend in and diminish my presence. It's exhausting. And horrible."

Fable's chest squeezed. She hated that she couldn't make things better for Thorn. She hated that people were wary of her friend and looked at her like a monster. And now, to discover this book filled with misinformation . . . Fable's magic vibrated inside her. For a moment, she wanted to unleash it at that book—no, at the whole store—for hurting her friend.

She clenched her teeth and forced her magic to still. *No. Letting the badness inside me out won't do anything but make this worse. I can't do that to Thorn.*

"I wish people weren't so cruel."

Thorn grasped Fable's hand. "Not everybody is. I know who I can trust."

The door behind them chimed. They twisted to see Fedilmid and Brennus approach. Both held large paper bags in their arms.

"Everything okay?" Fedilmid asked softly.

Thorn nodded. "We're fine."

The old witch pulled a wrinkly brown mushroom the size of his fist from his shopping bag. "I bought a few of these, Thorn. *Hydnum repandum*. They say these help with divination when brewed in a tea, but I hear they taste even better with a drizzle of butter and a dash of spice. I thought you could teach us how to cook them."

Thorn got to her feet with an eager look. "Hedgehog mushrooms! Where did they get these? They shouldn't be ready until late summer."

"They must have been grown indoors," Fedilmid replied. "Here, Fable, do you mind carrying this other bag for me?"

As Thorn chattered on about mushrooms and the value of using a cast iron pan over a steel one, Fable took the bag from Fedilmid. She peered inside and saw *The History of the Greenwood* tucked between sacks of herbs. She gave Fedilmid a questioning glance.

"I thought it'd be best to remove that one from public consumption," Fedilmid said quietly. "I'm sure it will make great fire-starter in the wood stove at the Thistle Plum."

Fable rested the bag on her hip. "Or bedding for Piper?"

"We wouldn't want him absorbing such abhorrent lies."

"Firestarter it is," Fable agreed.

As they made their way down the sidewalk, Fable couldn't help but think how lucky she was. Not only for the wonderful people in her life, but for the fact that she didn't face the scrutiny that Thorn did. For all anybody could see, she was just a normal girl. *Well, a normal girl with purple eyes.* But nobody seemed bothered by that.

Her magic tingled at her fingertips, reminding her of what lived inside her. If people only knew the truth. *The intimidating Folkvar is a peaceful person filled with light, and the plain little girl has darkness growing inside her that she can't control—ready to explode on anybody who comes too close.*

Secrets from the Past

Fable gazed over the white picket gate, surrounded by the sweet scent of lilacs. The bushes that lined the edge of the yard hung heavy with purple blooms. Pink buds that looked ready to burst into petals at any moment had replaced the autumnal orange leaves of the magnolia tree since the last time Fable had seen it. And at the end of the overgrown walkway sat the square stone cottage with the faded lavender door.

Home. Fable could hardly believe she was here, staring at the house that belonged to her. The house she had shared with her parents before her life had changed forever.

After the incident at The Arcane Scroll, the group from the Thistle Plum had gone their separate ways. Aunt Moira took Brennus and Timothy to Madam Mildred's for school supplies and to see if Ralazar's Odd & Unusual had returned yet. Not wanting another confrontation with Clarice, Thorn had opted to join Fedilmid and Fable.

Fedilmid gave the house an appreciative gaze. "It's a bit worn from sitting empty for so long. But it's nothing a little love and care won't fix up."

Thorn leaned back on her heels, her lips parted as she took in the home. "It's beautiful."

Fable kicked open the gate, which was stiff from the grass growing through the wooden slats. "Now that we have the key, we can actually go inside."

"Indeed," Fedilmid replied. He and Thorn followed her up the walkway. "It will be useful to see the layout and what needs the most attention for renovations this summer. With a little luck, you'll be able to move in before the fall."

Move in! A thread of giddy energy wound its way around Fable's heart. *My own home to share with my family and friends. In Mistford!*

When they reached the soft purple door, Fedilmid pulled a silver key from his pocket and slipped it into the lock. With a twist of his wrist, it clicked open and the group entered the home.

It was just as Fable remembered from last fall, when she had peered through the six-paned front window into the near-empty living room. A bulgy green couch sat along a wall with peeling floral wallpaper. The hardwood floor was scattered with shards of what must have been a vase or an ornamental pot. A thick layer of dust coated every nook and cranny.

A lump formed in Fable's throat. While Thorn and Fedilmid explored the house, commenting on this or that they could see being changed, she stepped through the living room and under an arched doorway into the simple, country-style kitchen. A round oak table sat in the spring sunshine that poured through the grimy window above the sink. She could imagine her mother sitting at that table with a warm cup of tea, scribbling in the journal that now lay inside Fable's book bag. She imagined her father whistling as he filled the kettle and put it on the stove to boil.

Fable's throat tightened. She fought back the tears that threatened to spill over.

Fedilmid called from the living room. "This floor is exceptional! The hardwood has hardly been scuffed at all. With a little magic, we'll have it up to shape in no time."

Fable wiped her cheek, then rejoined Fedilmid and Thorn in the living area. Fedilmid held his ear to the fireplace mantle. He gently tapped on a jagged grey rock. Thorn stood beside him, watching him with a confused look.

"What are you doing?" Fable asked.

"Checking for remnants of magic." Fedilmid hunched over to tap the stones near the base. "You never know what gets left behind in old houses. Energetic vibrations hum if you listen closely enough." He motioned towards the stairs beside the entryway. "Why don't you girls look upstairs? Fable, I bet your old bedroom is up there."

Fable and Thorn rushed up the wooden staircase that led to an open hallway with three doors. An empty bathroom sat behind the first door, but the second door opened to a brightly lit bedroom. Sunshine poured through the wide window, illuminating the pink walls. At the far end of the room sat an empty crib, stripped of its bedding.

Fable's chest fluttered. *This must have been my room.*

A bare oak bookcase stood in the far corner. Fable imagined it filled with the books now sitting in her and Timothy's tiny bedroom at Rose Cottage. The tense muscles in her neck relaxed. This room seemed familiar, like a memory tugging at her that she couldn't quite grasp.

Thorn stood in the doorway and swept her gaze over the room. She lowered her eyes, her expression solemn.

"Thorn?" Fable asked. "Are you okay?"

Thorn ran the end of her braid through her fingers. "I'm fine. I'm just emotional after what happened today. And being here makes me miss my home. It reminds me that, well, you know—that it's gone."

Fable hadn't thought of how her friend would react to seeing Fable's childhood cottage. *Of course this would make her sad.* Fable had roots, and family, and now a home of her own. Thorn's roots had gone up in flames along with the Greenwood Forest. She'd lost her home, her community, and her family. And she had just been reminded of it all at The Arcane Scroll.

Fable crossed the room to her friend's side. "I should have thought—"

"It's okay." Thorn held her hand in front of her, her face tight. "I don't want to talk about it anymore. Let's check out the other room."

"All right," Fable agreed. It was clear her friend wanted a change of topic, and Fable could understand that. Sometimes, the weight of everything that had happened because of Endora—to not only the Nuthatches, but to Thorn's and Brennus's families too—was too much to bear. With a quick nod in Thorn's direction, Fable led them into the hallway and to the last room.

Dust particles floated in the beam of sunlight that swept across the floor. Green floral wallpaper coated the walls. A fan hung from the ceiling. It was a typical adult bedroom, much like Aunt Moira's at Rose Cottage. Beside the four-poster bed against the far wall sat a nightstand with its drawer half-open.

Fable crossed the room to the side table and pulled the drawer open all the way. It was filled with stacks of papers. She pulled the top pages out, sat on the bed, and rifled through them. It was mostly old electrical bills and shopping receipts, but at the bottom of the pile was a folded piece of loose-leaf paper. Fable opened it and immediately recognized her mother's flowy handwriting. A photo, yellowed with age, slid onto her lap.

Thorn peered over her shoulder. "What is it? Is that—"

"My family," Fable whispered.

She gently picked up the photo and stared at it. A short, pretty woman with cheeks like ripe cherries and wavy brown hair smiled out at her. Beside her, a cheerful-looking man with shaggy, ink-black locks gazed at the toddler he held between them.

Fable's heart swelled in her chest. There was no mistaking the child's ebony hair that matched her father's, and the amethyst eyes that peered directly at the camera.

Her hands trembled as she lay the photo safely on the bed. She picked up the paper and began to read out loud.

Dearest Moira and Thomas,

We've had news that more people have gone miss-

ing in the Lichwood. Morton is certain it's Endora. Her powers are building, and we're afraid that she's going to use that horrible, final spell to complete her transformation. You know which one I'm talking about—the one that there's no coming back from.

I know you are busy building your lives and Thomas doesn't want anything to do with this. But we have to talk about it. At the very least, for the sake of our children. When yours arrives, he or she could be in danger too. Both of them need the love and protection we can provide together. We are stronger as a team.

Please, I ask you to consider what could happen to our families if we don't stop Endora. She wanted Thomas and she failed. But she's gaining strength. She's already tried once to take Fable. What if your child has magic too? Fable has brought more love and light into our lives than we ever thought possible. We would do absolutely anything to protect her. I know you feel the same way about your child. We must stop Endora before she rises to her full potential.

I've enclosed a family photo. Look at how much Fable has grown already! I don't want you to miss any more of her life. She deserves a loving aunty and uncle. So does your baby.

Please let us know a time that would work for you and Thomas to get together to discuss things. I hope we can come to a resolution and make amends.

Love and best wishes,

Faari, Morton, and Fable Nuthatch

Fable let her tears fall. *But why were they fighting? Because of Endora?* She skimmed the page again, now blurred through her watery eyes. And what did her mother mean by, *what could happen to our families if we don't stop Endora?* Obviously, Faari hadn't sent this to Moira. She must not have gotten the chance. What had happened that night her parents left her with her aunt? It was the last night both Fable and Moira had ever seen them, or Thomas, again.

Thorn glanced from the letter to Fable's face. "Are you okay?"

"I don't know." Fable's voice shook almost as hard as her hands. She folded the paper, tucked the photo inside, and slipped the bundle into her book bag between Faari's journal and the *Book of Chaos*. "I don't understand what this means. Aunt Moira has never told me much about my parents' deaths, or anything about Endora."

Thorn tilted her head. "Nothing about Endora at all?"

"Nothing. She thinks that pretending it isn't real will stop it from happening."

"Children?" Fedilmid's voice floated up the stairs.

"Are you ready to go?"

Fable looked up at her friend. "Please, don't tell him about this. I'm not ready to share." This was her story, part of her past. She needed time to mull things over.

Thorn drew her into a hug. "I promise I'll keep it a secret."

"Thank you." Fable hugged in return, then pulled away and wiped her cheeks. *Why is it up to me to unravel my past? Aunt Moira should have told me about this.*

They left the room and Fable closed the door behind her. Her heart ached as they thudded down the stairs. Her mother's words echoed inside her. *Fable has brought more love and light into our lives than we ever thought possible.*

As grateful as Fable was for her aunt's devotion to raising her, she hadn't told Fable any of these secrets about her past. About why her parents and Thomas died in that rockslide. Or about what Endora had been up to all those years ago, and how she became what she is now.

An ominous tingle wormed its way into Fable's chest.

Maybe she knows. Maybe she senses Endora's wicked spark hovering inside me, waiting to be un-

leashed. Fable's heart shrank to the corner of her chest. *No. I won't let the darkness take control of me.*

They reached the main floor of the house. Fedilmid opened the door and with a little bow he gestured towards the front yard. "Ready, girls?"

"You bet," Thorn replied.

Fable ran her hand over her book bag where the letter and photo lay. After a final glance behind her at the house she could now call her home, she followed her mentor and friend into the bright sunshine.

A Firehawk's Strangled Breath

Fable stood at the iron gate to the festival, taking in the newly transformed grounds. Willow arches with colourful ribbons entwined in the branches marked the entrances to the alley-ways, lined with open stalls and upright tents. With the Spring Festival only one day away, the place looked more like an enchanted forest than a carnival on a concrete square. The bright green Ferris wheel seemed starkly out of place in the mystical atmosphere, creaking as the bucket seats swung gently in the wind.

Thorn stepped up beside her. "Here come Moira and the boys."

Great.

Fable peered down the cobblestone sidewalk. Brennus's lean frame sauntered along beside Moira and Timothy, who were holding hands. At the thought of talking to her aunt, a pit formed in her stomach. How could she pretend everything was okay after what she'd read in her mother's letter that afternoon?

After their visit to Eighteen Lilac Avenue, Fedilmid had dropped Thorn and Fable off at the fairgrounds so they could meet up with the others. He then rushed off to meet Algar at the building supply shop at the other end of town.

The trio from Tulip Manor reached the gate. Aunt Moira gripped Timothy's hand in hers. His ashen face was contorted into a grimace of pain.

Fable's stomach twinged. *He must have been hit with another headache.*

Aunt Moira squeezed his hand tighter and flicked her gaze to Fable. "Timothy isn't feeling well. I think it's best if we all go back together." She glanced over her shoulder as if expecting Endora to be standing right behind her. "You just never know who's lurking about."

"We're not babies," Fable replied. She heard the snap in her voice, but did nothing to alter it as she continued. "Besides, there are plenty of people around. Do you really think Endora or her henchman would be out in public in the middle of the afternoon?"

Aunt Moira raised her eyebrows at Fable's tone. "No, but—"

Thorn gave Moira a pleading look. "Please, Moira. I really want to see if my sister is here."

At that, Aunt Moira softened. "Of course you do,

dear."

She turned to her niece, her hands on her hips, and her expression hardened into a familiar *don't-mess-this-up* look. "Stick together. And get to the Thistle Plum before dark. Not *at* dark. Not five minutes *after* dark. *Before* dark."

"What if we walk in right as the sun is setting?" Brennus asked.

Aunt Moira let go of Timothy's hand and crossed her arms. "You know what I mean. I'm serious. This is your chance to prove to me that you've learned your lesson, and you won't follow your noses into any more trouble. Don't blow it."

Relief washed over Fable as her aunt and Timothy walked away. Now she and her friends were free to search the fairgrounds without Aunt Moira's constant hovering—and she had more time to think about what to say to her aunt about the letter.

The friends strolled through the fairgrounds towards the towering big top, watching the vendors hastily hang their flags, arrange merchandise, and set up wooden signposts. Fable admired the colourful flowers that lined the stalls and the gadgets vendors were hanging from their awnings. Behind her, Brennus and Thorn had started bickering. She caught something about Brennus's guitar and the Folkvars, and her ears perked up.

"That's not how the guitar works." Brennus said in exasperation. "And I've never been to the Burntwood. That book says I have to think clearly about where I want to go. How can I envision somewhere I've never been?"

"Why can't you just try?" Thorn asked.

"I could end up in Stonebarrow. Or the Burning Sands. Or who knows where. Last time I landed in the coffee shop in Firdale."

"It's just a projection. It's not like you were actually transported there."

"You should have seen the look on the barista's face when a bright purple light with a boy inside it burst into the line. And what was I supposed to do? Ask for a caramel macchiato?"

"I'll do it, then. You just need to tell me what to do," Thorn insisted.

Brennus hesitated, then his voice quieted. "I haven't figured out what to do. Besides, we can't trust it. You could get hurt."

A couple, dressed in clown costumes and walking on stilts, approached the children. The gentleman took off his velvet top hat and gave them a tipsy bow. He handed Brennus a lollipop and then continued on his way. Brennus took the candy with barely a glance.

"Thanks." He unwrapped the lollipop and stuck it in his mouth.

Fable watched the pair wobble away. *Will I ever get used to these strange and wonderful events in Mistford?* Larkmoor's Harvest Festival had been nothing like this. There had been one lane of rough wooden stalls that mostly comprised of boring games that involved throwing a ball at pop bottles. It had none of the magic of this place.

Of course, everybody there hates magic. Period.

Thorn caught up to her, twirling her sister's arrow in her fingers. "Do you think Endora would come to the festival? She probably knows we'd come here for it. And if she's looking for Fable to complete her spell—"

"Doubt it." Brennus swivelled the lollipop to his other cheek. "It's not like her to do her own dirty work. But she would probably send her new henchman—that stinky guy. What was his name? Dwight?"

"Doug." Fable turned this information over in her mind as they stepped through an ornate archway that led to the alley with the big top tent at the very end.

Brennus pulled the treat from his mouth and smirked. "If we come across a trail of dirt and muddy footprints, we'll know he's around."

"That, and the lingering stench of graveyard."

Thorn pointed the arrow at the dirt.

Brennus snorted a laugh.

When they got close to the striped big-top that would host the games, hundreds of knee-high mushrooms with red-and-white polka dotted caps lined the sides of the walkway.

Thorn held the arrow with one hand and bent to examine the fungi. "These are real! *Amanita muscaria*. How did they get so huge?"

"Of course they're real. They hire the best witches to decorate the place," Brennus replied.

"Well, whatever you do, don't eat them." Thorn straightened and gave them a serious look. "You'll think you're walking on the moon."

"That doesn't sound so bad," Brennus said.

Thorn raised a brow. "You say that now. But it would be different later, when everything you ate during that day comes back up."

Brennus looked as if he'd smelled something vile. "Gross."

"Why do they use witches to decorate and not sorceresses or wizards?" Fable asked.

"Witches are good with plants and fungi and things like that," Brennus replied. "Like Alice. Or Fedilmid. I wonder if he ever worked for the carnival when he

161

was young."

Fable had no idea. She didn't know much about Fedilmid's past at all—only that he'd left his home as a young man to come to Starfell. She didn't even know where he had lived before he planted his roots at Tulip Manor. A thorn of guilt pricked her spine. He had done so much for her, and she had never even asked him about his life. She vowed to fix that.

When they reached the entrance to the striped tent, they passed a trio of musicians who were leaving the building. A man with a bald head as shiny as the glass orbs at the Arcane Scroll lead the way with a flute in his hands. A stout woman who couldn't have been any taller than Fable followed him holding a mandolin, and a young boy no older than Timothy trailed after her, his burgundy robes dragging on the ground and a cedar guitar strapped around his neck.

Brennus gave them a look of longing. "Toby's parents are letting him play now. Back when we travelled together, Mom always told Mrs. Finch that he'd make a great guitarist."

The boy grinned and waved at Fable and her friends. Brennus gave him a nod and watched them wistfully as they walked away.

"Brennus?" Fable asked gently.

"My parents must be missing this. We played this festival every year," he said, his gaze on the guitarist's back. "No wonder the Odd and Unusual Shop hasn't been in Mistford lately. Mom must have directed the store away from here."

"She'd need the guitar to do that."

"Maybe she found another way. *She's a genius*, remember?" Brennus gave a weak smile at the quote from his father. "If we can get the guitar to work—"

"Then we can all try—" Thorn stopped abruptly and pointed at a line of cages that were stacked in the shadow of the big-top. "Are those firehawks?"

Fable followed Thorn's gaze to the animal enclosures. When she'd first seen them from Nightwind's back, the cages had been empty. Today, they were filled with creatures of all imaginable shapes and sizes. A spotted cat with tufts on the tips of its ears paced behind a set of iron bars. A group of lime-green birds with hooked beaks and spindly legs like flamingos crowded together in the cage beside it. Two horse-sized wolves stared at them from the next enclosure. Their scarlet eyes sent a tremor through Fable.

Endora's hounds have eyes like that.

At the end of the line, next to a stack of empty wooden crates that stood taller than Thorn, sat a cage the size of a large dog kennel. Several mottled brown, chicken-like birds were lying inside it in a fluffy pile of feathers and moss-green spots. One of the hens raised its head and stared in the trio's direction. She let out a soft cluck.

"Fable?" The bird blinked in surprise.

Fable's heart jumped to her throat. "Star!"

She rushed to the cage that contained the birds. An iron lock hung from the latch on the door. Gripping the wire mesh side, she knelt and peered inside.

"Star, is that really you?"

Star shook herself free of the bird pile and approached Fable. Her feathers were ruffled and dirty, and her feet were caked with mud and straw.

"Fable, dear! I thought I'd never see you again. I have so much to tell you—"

Four little heads popped up from the mound of feathers.

"Human!"

"Girl!"

"Bwaak!" One of them opened her mouth as if to blow fire, but only exuded a puff of smoke and a strangled cry.

That didn't seem right. They were called fire-hawks for a reason. Star never had an issue using her fire breath before. In fact, the only problem she had was containing it. It was then that Fable noticed the silver chain wrapped snuggly around the throat of the firehawk whose head was surrounded by smoke. Star had one too, right where her leather pouch should have been. Fable glanced at the other firehawks. All four of them wore the same shackles.

Star craned her neck at them and hissed. "She's a friend, ladies! Can you not sense her aura?"

The other hens tittered and clucked. They shrank closer together and stared at Fable with white-rimmed eyes.

Star let out a low cluck. "Poor dears, they're terrified. Don't know up from down since the incident. I try to remain hopeful, but things keep getting bleaker the further we get from home."

Fable's magic roused inside her, a slow burn ready to erupt at the first spark of emotion. Fable gritted her teeth. *No! I will not allow myself to hurt Star like I did Grimm.*

From behind her, Thorn spoke up. "What happened to you? What's around your throat?"

The firehawk stretched her neck with an awkward tilt. "I'm afraid it's enchanted. The magic stops our fire breath. He takes them off only for the show, and by

then our throats are burning from holding it in all day."
She glanced at the trembling hens behind her. "The one
whose aura smells like a mountain meadow—her fire is
failing. It grows weaker every day." She leaned in closer to Fable and quieted her voice. "Who knows what
he's going to do with her if she stops performing."

Anger boiled in the pit of Fable's stomach, leach-
ing into her magic. Sweat formed on her brow. "Who
is he? Who did this to you?"

Star peeked over Fable's shoulder, then stepped
closer to the wire and nuzzled her fingers. "I heard
somebody call him Aldric Crane. He owns this show,
the Magical Menagerie." She gestured to the other cages with her wing. "He's captured all sorts of creatures
from around Starfell. From the Burning Sands and the
Burntwood, even the Windswept Mountains. He's able
to control our magic." Her voice broke. "We were out
scrounging for dew worms, minding our own business,
when—"

"*Fwap!*" one of the other hens piped up. "A net
swooped up from the ground and yanked us into the
air."

"It burned," the firehawk beside that one said, bob-
bing her head, "and it choked the fire breath from us."

The third firehawk threw her head back and wailed.

166

"And ever since then we've been stuck in this cage! We're only allowed out to perform—"

"Ssh!" Star hissed at them and stamped her taloned feet. "If he hears us, he'll chase the dear child off and we'll never get out of here."

The wrath inside Fable climbed to her chest. Her magic throbbed, pushing at her edges and searching for the spark. She looked at the other magical creatures. The spotted cat watched her curiously, but the flamingo-like birds and the wolves had little interest in her. Their misery hung heavy in the air like a blanket of despair.

Fable took a deep breath. *How are we going to get them out of here without causing complete chaos?*

Brennus must have been reading her mind. "Let me pick the lock," he said from behind her.

Fable glanced over her shoulder. Brennus and Thorn stood side by side. Brennus had his multi-tool in his hand with the lock pick extended from the handle. He gestured towards the cage with it.

Thorn crossed her arms over her chest. "I'll keep watch."

Fable wiped the sweat from her brow, barely containing the surge of magic within her. She looked at the firehawks. "My friend Brennus is going to trade places with me and get you out. He's safe. He has a tool that can help."

Star narrowed her eyes at Brennus. "Aren't you the boy who stole Fable's coins at the Buttertub? The one who caused all that fuss—"

"It's okay," Fable said. "He's my friend."

One of Star's flockmates ruffled her wings. "I don't know about this."

"Can he be trusted?"

"Ssh!"

Fable stood aside. Brennus shoved his canvas bag behind his back, then knelt by the cage door. He spun the pick in his hand and inserted it into the keyhole.

The tingles of power curled around Fable's spine, settled like a serpent coiling in its basket. For now.

She glanced at Thorn, who blocked the empty alleyway with her large frame. *Anybody could come around that corner at any minute, and there's no way we could hide. It's broad daylight.*

"Brennus—" she started.

A raspy voice clanged through the air like a screeching train. "Hey! What are you kids doing to my firehawks?"

A broad man with arms almost as big as Thorn's marched towards them, his face as red as a ripe chili pepper.

Thorn stood between her friends and the angry man, doing her best to block them from his view. "We're just looking at them."

The man's spine straightened and he cast Thorn a wary glance. "You can look at them from ten paces back!"

"We need to see them up close," Thorn said in a steady voice. "For school. We're doing a report on them for science."

The man, presumably Aldric, balled his hands into fists. His mouth twisted into an angry scowl and his brows furrowed so deeply that Fable wondered how he could see through the creases. He gave Thorn's bulky frame a sideways glance. "Tell your friends to back off, or I'll make them!"

Brennus jiggled the lock pick frantically. "I can't get it! It must be enchanted."

The firehawks squawked in distress. Star pressed herself up against the cage. "Please hurry, dear!"

Time seemed to slow for Fable. Brennus's frenzied energy and Aldric's rage whirled in the air like an on-coming storm. A storm that pushed at Fable's magic, trying to find a way in. Her tingles turned into full-blown panic.

Use your magic! Make a shield. She took a deep breath and rubbed her hands together, trying to focus on building a protective barrier around her friends at the cage. Fedilmid's words whispered in her head. *Work with your emotions. Let your light outshine the darkness.*

A blue shimmer sparked in her palms.

The man stood toe-to-toe with Thorn, his face crimson. Spittle flew from his lips. "I'm giving you one more chance!"

Thorn widened her stance and re-crossed her arms. "Look, sir—"

"Brennus!" Fable hissed. Her stomach clenched. They had to get Star out. She couldn't leave her feathered friend behind in that awful cage.

Sweat shone from Brennus's forehead as he twisted the metal pick back and forth. He smacked the lock against the latch. "I can't get it. It's magic!"

Thorn's voice grew louder. "Sir, please, calm down."

"And why would I listen to likes of you?" the man growled. "I know how you people are. Trying to steal my firehawks, aren't ya? I won't stand for it!"

Another voice, softer and quieter, came from behind Thorn and Aldric. "Ex-excuse me, p-perhaps I can help."

Fable peered around Thorn to see Malcolm approach with a hitched step. His long black robe dragged on the ground around his feet. For a moment, Fable thought he was going to trip.

What's he doing here? She thought of the bird skull from his box at the Thistle Plum. *Was that a firehawk? Is he helping Aldric?*

Aldric either didn't hear Malcolm or completely ignored him. "You don't want me getting my boss involved, Folkvar," he sneered. "You don't want to be on Ralazar's bad side."

Ralazar!

Brennus's head shot up. The lock pick fell from his fingers.

What does Ralazar have to do with this? Fable swept her gaze from the huddling firehawks to the spotted cat, who now cowered in the back of its enclosure. *Did he order the capture of these creatures?*

Star let out a strangled sob, and a powerful shot of chaotic emotion hit Fable like a puff of fire breath, though no flame came from Star's beak. The air was forced from Fable's lungs. Emerald flames danced down her forearms and poured from her sleeves.

No!

Brennus froze, staring at the green flames with a look of horror on his face. He flicked his gaze to Fable and snapped his jaw shut.

"N-now, Aldric." Malcolm had his back to the children, unaware of the danger that had just erupted a few feet behind him.

Thorn narrowed her eyes at the flames, then whirled towards the pile of wooden crates beside him. She grabbed one from the middle of the pile with both hands and heaved. The stack rocked precariously.

"Stop!" Aldric stepped forward, his hands in the air. But it was too late.

Thorn heaved on the crates again. The whole pile groaned and tilted, then toppled down in a roaring crash. Thorn leapt out of the way just in time. A pile of broken crates lie between them and the adults.

Fable's green flames tore towards the splintered wood and they ignited with a roar.

Thorn grabbed her friends' hands, jerking Brennus to his feet. He grabbed his multi-tool from the ground, shoved it into his bag, and they ran.

The flock of firehawks shrieked hysterically behind them. Fable's heart curled in shame. She looked over her shoulder. Star pressed up against the cage, watching them run away.

"Star! We'll come back." Fable choked on the words. "I promise!"

Aldric stomped on the flames, waving his arms and screaming in a fit of rage. Malcolm ran towards him with a bucket of sloshing water.

We have to come back. Fable fought back a sob as she struggled to keep up with Thorn's long strides. The spell list popped into her mind.

Flame of a firehawk's last breath.

Trapped in that cage, Star and her friends were easy targets for Endora. Fable knew in her heart that her great-grandmother would hunt them down here, lured by her obsession with the power of the Blood Star.

And with my horrible flames and uncontrollable darkness, I just made things so much worse.

Despite her tormenting thoughts and heart begging her to turn back for the firehawks, Fable forced herself to follow her friends through the gate and into the streets of Mistford.

The Guitar of Mayhem

Star is never going to forgive me. Fable's chest pinched with guilt as she and her friends ran up the winding street towards the inn. The shadows of the hedges beside the sidewalk stretched across their path, the sky painted the dusky blue hue that signaled night was soon to come.

Aunt Moira's voice rang in her ears. *This is your chance to prove to me that you've learned your lesson. Don't blow it.* She would never let Fable and her friends out of her sight again if they were late. Fable willed her tired legs to keep going as the trio crashed through the iron gate and into the overgrown yard of the Thistle Plum. They stumbled up the creaky steps of the porch, Thorn yanked open the door and they piled into the entryway.

"We made it!" Thorn said.

Brennus straightened his hooded sweatshirt, breathing heavily. "Just . . . in . . . time."

Fable righted her book bag around her hip and gripped the hard edge of her mother's journal through the fabric.

"Children?" Aunt Moira's voice came from the dining area. "Is that you?"

Fable's heart squeezed. She thought of the letter that was tucked inside her book bag and her feelings of anger and sadness from that afternoon came flooding back. The last thing she wanted to do right now was to talk to her aunt. *Besides, I don't have time for this now. We need to make a plan to save Star!*

"Yes, Aunt Moira!" She caught Brennus's eye and jerked her head towards the staircase. "Upstairs," she whispered. "To Thorn's and my room."

Brennus nodded. "I'll grab my guitar."

"Alice has butternut squash soup on, if you're interested," Aunt Moira called.

"We're going to wash up. We'll be down in a bit."

"All right, then," Moira replied. "Don't be too long or it'll be all gone. And try not to wake Timothy. Grimm's up there with him."

Relief washed over Fable as they climbed the stairs. They'd done it. *Well, sort of.* They'd made it back to the Thistle Plum before dark, but they hadn't kept out of trouble. *Aunt Moira doesn't need to know about that.*

Thorn and Fable slipped into their room and sat on Thorn's bed. Brennus joined them there a few minutes later with his guitar in hand. He slipped his canvas bag from his shoulder, placed it in the armchair across from them, and plopped down next to it. With a frown of concentration, he fiddled with the tuning pegs on the headstock of his instrument.

Exhaustion crept over Fable, and she fought back a yawn. So much had happened that day, and it finally caught up to her. The visit to the ministry, the incidents at the Arcane Scroll, the letter and photo from her mother to Aunt Moira, and the heartbreaking image of her captured friend circled Fable's thoughts. *And we still haven't seen any sign of Orchid.*

She closed her eyes. Emerald flames flickered at the corners of the darkness in her mind. She popped her eyes open and stared at her friends. "I started a fire!"

Thorn cocked a brow. "So, I take it your flames aren't just some trick Fedilmid taught you?"

Brennus gave Fable a wary glance. "Well, I mean, they turned out to be a good thing."

Fable's stomach lurched. He'd looked so shocked when she'd started that fire. *I scared him.*

Thorn pulled the broken arrow from her vest and

tapped it against the palm of her hand. "Never mind that right now. We have to save those firehawks."

"And not only for Star, but for all of Starfell," Brennus said. "You read what that curse will do to the star."

"It's not like Endora couldn't find other firehawks," Thorn said darkly.

"No, but we can help these ones," Fable said through a lump in her throat. She pictured Star and her flock huddled together in their cage with chains around their necks. Even if Endora wasn't after them, she had to get them out of there. Her shoulders slumped.

"I can't believe I left them."

"It wasn't your fault. If Aldric hadn't come—" Thorn started.

"No." Brennus shook his head. "I should have got that lock open. I can't do anything right. Between that and this stupid guitar"—he thumped the side of it—"I'm useless."

"You're not," Fable said. "You just don't have magic. It's not your fault."

"Did you hear that guy mention Ralazar?" Brennus asked. "He's got to be working for the warlock. The same as my parents."

"And Malcolm." Thorn pointed the arrow towards the door. "He must be involved somehow."

Fable worried the sleeve of her dress between her fingers. Why was Malcolm at the fairgrounds today? He seemed to know Aldric. With his collection of bird skulls and rat hides, could he be a collector of magical creatures too?

"We should tell Fedilmid," Thorn said. "He'll want to help Star."

"And risk him telling Aunt Moira? We'll be kept under lock and key in this inn for the rest of the trip." Brennus shot back. "We'll never save Star that way. Or find Sir Reinhard. Or Orchid."

"We won't find Orchid anyways, at this rate." Thorn's face reddened. "We'd have to get into the games tent at the fairgrounds first. And you won't even try to look for her with that guitar."

"How?" Brennus glared at her. "That's not how the guitar works. It's not a magic Folkvar detector."

He pulled the sparkly book from his canvas bag. "According to this, we have to envision where we are going. We have no idea where Orchid is. She might not even be in Mistford. We don't know for sure—"

"You refuse to even try! You're so caught up with yourself—"

Brennus twisted a tuning key and purple light sparked in its sound hole.

Thorn raised the arrow in his direction. "Careful."

"I know what I'm doing."

"Do you?" Thorn jerked the arrow through the air. "Because last time I checked, you still haven't been able to contact your parents."

"What's crawled up your nose today?" Brennus strummed an angry chord. A purple glow flashed across the body of the vine-covered instrument. "This guitar's none of your business."

Their anger pulsed through the air like heat waves from a volcano. Fable's hands grew clammy. *This is not helping.*

"Guys—" she interjected.

Thorn shook the arrow at him with a scowl that would stop even the bravest knight in their tracks. "It's related to Orchid's bow, isn't it? You haven't thought for one minute that it could help us find her."

Brennus's jaw dropped. Wordlessly, he glowered at Thorn, turned another key, and then strummed again.

The vines on the guitar lit up in a golden glow. Purple smoke poured from the sound hole.

"I can't listen to you two bickering for one more second!" Fable jumped to her feet, snatched the arrow from Thorn's hand, and then marched over to Brennus to do the same with his guitar. As soon as her fingers

179

touched its neck, purple smoke snaked around her. The floor rocked beneath her feet and she fell, plummeting through a vibrant amethyst vortex.

Fable gasped for air, wondering if she'd ever be able to breathe again. Her stomach felt as though she'd been sucker-punched. Her head swam with the remnants of violet light. She forced her eyes open, but it made little difference—her surroundings were pitch black.

She sat up on the concrete floor and tried to get her bearings. A faint amethyst glow surrounded her, casting a soft illumination on her immediate surroundings. It was a small comfort in the otherwise near-perfect darkness. She strained to see something of her surroundings. Wherever she was, it smelled musty, and something faintly dripped nearby.

She tried to wipe her palms on the skirt of her dress. But instead of meeting fabric over solid thighs, her hands went right through. Orchid's broken arrow was nowhere to be seen.

Then, she remembered the purple smoke pouring over her from Brennus's guitar. *I must be astral projecting! Just like Brennus's mom did last fall when we saw her in the Lichwood!*

A bright light sparked in the darkness from some distance away. She squinted at it. The light flared and settled into the shape of glowing golden vines twisting around the handle of a bow.

Orchid!

By the soft light emitted by the vines, she could see the bow resting on a cluttered table near a concrete wall. Fable pushed her astral-self to her feet and approached it.

The glowing bow lay among several other objects and trinkets scattered on the rough wooden table. The vines that wound around the weapon's handle matched the vines on Brennus's guitar and her *Book of Chaos*. She automatically grabbed for her book bag, but her hands met nothing but wisps of air.

How did this happen? All I did was touch the guitar. Somehow, the bow must have called to the instrument. Had her magic sparked the connection?

She moved her gaze to the other objects on the table. The skull of a small rodent lay near the bow's string. A sword rested on the back edge of the table, glinting in the light from the bow. A stained and wrinkled pamphlet lay crumpled beside the blade.

She leaned forward to read the words printed in bold red letters across the top. *The Order of the Jade Antlers.*

Fable wrinkled her brow. *The Jade Antlers? What does that mean?*

The door creaked open. Fable whirled around to see a lanky Folkvar girl with waist-length copper hair step into the room. The girl stopped abruptly and locked her moss-green eyes with Fable's.

"Who are you?" she demanded. She glanced at the glowing bow on the table next to Fable, her hands ready for action.

Fable stared at her, frozen to the spot. *Orchid! At last! But what's she doing here?*

The silhouette of a robed figure appeared behind the girl, but before Fable could scream, a familiar hook-nosed man with scraggly black hair pushed his way into the room. "O-orchid, what are you d-doing?" He looked at Fable and his eyes grew wide. "F-Fable?"

Fable opened her mouth to speak, but the amethyst light around her flared and the air squeezed in tight around her.

Everything went black.

FIFTEEN

Darkness Falls

F able blinked and the worried faces of Thorn and Brennus came into focus above her. She was back at the Thistle Plum, laying on her bed with a quilt tucked to her chin.

"Wh-what happened?" She sat up and rubbed her throbbing forehead.

Thorn put a comforting hand on her shoulder. "You should lay down. You were totally out of it for a few minutes."

"Out of it?"

"Completely zonked!" Brennus gaped at her. "The same way my dad described my mom when she astral projected, just staring blankly into space. I couldn't pull you out of it. But luckily Thorn shook you hard enough—"

"I didn't shake her," Thorn interjected.

Brennus gave her a sideways glance. "Well, you grabbed her shoulders and, uh, *wiggled her around*."

Thorn gave him a jab to his shoulder.

"Ow!" Brennus rubbed his arm. "I guess that was just a love tap, not a thump, then?"

Thorn rolled her eyes.

Fable pushed the blanket from her lap. "What happened?"

"Why don't you tell us?" Brennus cast a wary glance at the guitar, which now looked as innocent as the chair it was propped up on. The broken arrow lay on the floor next to it. "You grabbed Orchid's arrow, touched the guitar, and then snapped straight into zombie mode."

Fable shuddered. She didn't like the thought of herself staring into space like one of Endora's undead—minus the black cloak and gaunt features—

She bolted upright. "Malcolm!"

"Malcolm?" Thorn raised her brows.

It all came rushing back. The dingy basement, the bow on the table, the trinkets and the sword, and the pamphlet that read *The Order of the Jade Antlers*. And, most importantly, Orchid and Malcolm. The whole story tumbled out of her like water spilling over a dam.

When Fable was done, she curled her knees to her chest and hugged them. "It was really weird. I couldn't touch anything, even myself. I guess only my thoughts were there."

Her friends stared at her.

She swallowed. "You believe me, don't you?"

"Of course." Thorn scratched the back of her neck. "It's just—"

"I'd been working on that guitar for months," Brennus said with a glum look. "And just like that"—he snapped his fingers—"you made it work."

"And I've been desperate to see Orchid," Thorn added. "We're just a bit jealous, I guess."

Fable's heart squeezed in her chest. "I didn't even try to make it happen. I can't help that my magic does whatever it wants, whenever it wants. I wish I had control of it!"

Thorn's face crumpled and Brennus ran his hand through his hair, avoiding Fable's gaze.

Fable immediately regretted her sharp tone. "I'm sorry."

Thorn heaved a sigh and took a seat next to Fable. "It's okay. Now we have something to work with. Did Orchid look okay?"

Fable nodded, her tension easing. "She looked perfectly fine. Except why is she staying in a grungy old basement? And why was she with Malcolm? I thought she'd be staying at the fairgrounds."

Thorn's brow creased with worry. "Did it look like Malcolm had captured her? She's tough, but if he has strong magic, like Endora . . ."

"No, she didn't seem like she was in trouble."

"Maybe he's got her under a spell of some kind?" Brennus suggested. "Was she in zombie mode like you were?"

Fable shook her head. "No, she was aware of what was going on. I think I scared her."

"She probably thought she was going crazy."

"I remember how strange it was when we saw Brennus's mom astral project in the Lichwood." Thorn stared at the floor. "And at least Brennus knew her. She has no idea who you are, Fable."

They were silent for a moment. Fable was sure Thorn's mind must have been racing as hard as hers. Her heart ached for her friend. Of course she was jealous. *Orchid is her sister, and I was the one to find her first. Well, sort of. I still have no idea where she is.*

"What's the Order of the Jade Antlers?" Brennus scratched his chin. "I've never heard of it before."

"You know, we could just ask Malcolm." Thorn said. "He's staying right down the hall."

Brennus screwed up his face. "Just ask him why he's hanging out with a firehawk kidnapper and your missing sister? No way."

The Order of the Jade Antlers. Fable had no idea why, but the name tugged at her. Maybe it was in a book she'd read at Rose Cottage? Or something Fedilmid had mentioned to her in their lessons?

"What do you think, Fable?" Thorn asked. "Do you think Malcolm seems trustworthy? He's a bit different, but he seemed nice enough. He could have just been walking by the cages at the fairground and heard the commotion. If he's friends with Orchid, he must be okay."

"Maybe." Fable wasn't sure what to think of the scraggly-haired man. He was odd, but that didn't mean bad. And Thorn was right, he could have been at the fair by coincidence.

But why hadn't he mentioned to Thorn that he knew another Folkvar? *It's not like they're common around here.*

Brennus picked up *Astral Projecting for Fledgling Wizards* from his bag on the floor. He wiped the glittery cover with his sleeve. "You could try to project again. See if you can speak to Orchid."

Thorn scratched her chin, a troubled look on her face. "Do you think it's safe? Now that I've seen Fable do it—well, I was afraid she wasn't going to come back."

"We have this to help us now." Brennus waved the book in Thorn's direction.

"No." Fable tugged at her sleeve. "To be honest, I wasn't sure I'd come back either. The whole thing was so confusing. What if I end up somewhere else—like

Endora's mansion?"

Brennus lowered the book. "I guess you're right. I read in one of Fedilmid's books that magical objects created from the same energy often forge a connection. Endora created all those Collectors. I bet they're linked. And there are dozens of them right inside her lair."

Thorn nodded. "We can't risk sending you there, Fable."

Fable's thoughts circled back to the hook-nosed man. "We need to find Malcolm. Tomorrow when we see him here, we can follow him and see where he goes. I bet he'll go to either the Magical Menagerie or lead us to Orchid. Or both."

"I like it," Brennus said.

"What if he catches us?" Thorn asked.

"He won't," Brennus replied. "We'll be careful."

"When have we ever been careful?"

A knock sounded at the door followed by Aunt Moira's voice. "Children?"

"Hide the book!" Fable hissed at Brennus. "We don't want her to think we were trying to astral project. She'll lock us in the Thistle Plum forever. And she'll take the book and your guitar."

He thrust it beneath the armchair. "It's gone."

Thorn stood, grabbed the pillow from her bed, and jammed it under the chair. "*Now* it's gone."

Fable opened the door. Her aunt stood in the hallway holding a tray with three bowls of vibrant orange soup. "I thought you children might want a bite before we put away the leftovers for Fedilmid and Algar."

Fable stepped aside and let her into the room. "Thanks. They aren't back yet?"

"Not yet. I imagine they ran in to some friends downtown."

Aunt Moira greeted Thorn and Brennus. She set the tray on the table beside the armchair. "Fedilmid raved on about how much he loved Alice's butternut squash soup, so we made sure to save a few bowls for them." She motioned to the tray she had just set down, saw the pillow under the back of the chair, and tilted her head. "I just reheated these for you."

"Thank you," Thorn and Brennus chorused brightly. Thorn casually moved her foot in front of the pillow and propped her elbow on the back of the chair, resting her chin on her first and grinning like she hadn't a care in the world.

Moira frowned at the pillow. "Thorn, why—?"

Fable swallowed in alarm. "Aunt Moira?"

Moira snapped her gaze from the pillow to Fable. "Yes, dear?"

Fable glanced around the room, trying to think of something to say. She spotted her book bag hanging from the four-poster bed behind Thorn and remembered the letter.

She grabbed the bag's strap and lifted it from the bedpost. She looked at her aunt. "Can we talk outside?"

Aunt Moira shot her a curious glance, but nodded. "Sure." She placed the third bowl of soup on the table, then took hold of the tray with one hand and led the way out of the room. Before she went through the door, she called over her shoulder. "Thorn, pick up that pillow, please. We don't want to ruin Alice's linens."

"Yes, ma'am," Thorn said.

Fable glanced at her friend, whose blue-grey skin had flushed lavender.

Thank you, mouthed Brennus.

Fable gave him a nod, then followed her aunt out of the room. She wasn't sure she was ready for this conversation, but she'd committed now.

Once they were in the hallway, Fable closed the door behind them and wiped her hands on her dress, as if she could rub away her nerves.

"Is something the matter?" Aunt Moira readjusted the tray against her hip.

Fable's pulse raced at the thought of confronting her aunt about the letter, but she had to know more. She untied the string of her bag and rifled through it until she found the folded paper. She handed it to Aunt Moira. "I found this at my house today."

Her aunt unfolded the letter. The photo slid from its creases, but her aunt caught it before it could fall. Her eyes widened as she scanned the paper.

"Well?" Fable crossed her arms.

Aunt Moira swallowed. Her voice softened. "Well, what?"

"Well, what do you have to say about this?" Fable asked. "Why didn't you tell me that you and my parents didn't get along? That you didn't want to help fight Endora? And, clearly, didn't want me in your life?"

That wasn't fair and Fable knew it. But her emotions swept her up like a raging river, her mouth as out-of-control as her magic had been earlier.

Tears sprang to Aunt Moira's eyes. Her chin trembled. "You don't know about everything that happened. We were trying to keep Thomas and Timothy safe. Timothy wasn't even born yet and Endora was already a danger to him."

"Exactly! I *don't* know." Fable gave her an accusatory stare. "You haven't told me anything about my past. And hardly a thing about my parents."

"That's not true."

Fable snorted. "Sure, I know my mom loved plants and my dad loved books. I know they craved adventure and were brave enough to stand up against Endora.

But you've never told me why they had to in the first place—why they had to die."

"Oh, Fable." Aunt Moira reached out with her free arm to pull her into a hug but Fable backed away.

"All this time, I thought you were close with my parents. That you loved them." Heat washed over Fable's cheeks. Her magic swelled in her veins. "Now I find out that you didn't want anything to do with them. Or me. But you got stuck with me. I'm sure you wish they'd left me with Endora."

Aunt Moira lifted her chin. Pangs of hurt and confusion permeated the air around them.

"That's not true. I took you in because I love you. Thomas and I both loved your parents fiercely, but his and Timothy's lives were at risk from Endora. We wanted a safe life for our family. And things changed. That night they left for the Lichwood . . . well, we'd made up. We were a team again."

Fable's fingers cramped with the effort to hold her magic at bay. The hurt, anger, and betrayal were so overwhelming that she could barely hold it all in. "Why have you hidden all of this from me? Why haven't you told me what happened in our family? This is my life too!"

"You may not think so, but you're still a child." Aunt Moira's voice shook. "I am still your guardian and have final say in the decisions about your life. I want what's best for you. I want to keep you alive!"

"That doesn't answer anything!" Fable tossed her hands in the air in frustration. Purple sparks crackled between her fingers.

Aunt Moira's back stiffened and she took a step away from Fable. "We will talk about this later, once you have calmed down. You're in no state to discuss such personal matters right now." The tremor in her voice betrayed her calm expression.

Fable's heart sank. *She's afraid of me. First, I scared Brennus. Now, my own aunt.*

"You think my magic's going to go off and kill us, don't you?" Fable choked on the words. Her emotions pulsed through the hallway, and by the look on Aunt Moira's face, Fable was sure the witch could feel them too.

I'm dangerous. I'm dark, like Endora.

With a sob, she slung her book bag over her shoulder and fled down the stairs.

"Fable!" Aunt Moira called after her.

Fable shook her head, letting the tears stream down her face. She ran out of the Thistle Plum and into the starry night.

SIXTEEN

Feathers and Scales

Fable ran through the tall grass towards Nightwind's stable. Barbed nettles snatched at her leggings. The full moon hung in the sky like a yule ornament on a tree, illuminating the new tin roof and grey stones of the building. She raced to the wooden door, slid it open, and slipped inside.

She flicked on the light. Nightwind's velvety nose reached over the half-door of his stall. His ears perked forward and he let out a soft whinny as she approached. His wings, folded against his body, shimmered in the soft light. Between the pterippus's body heat and the fresh straw on the floor, it was cozy and warm in the one-stall barn. Fable couldn't have asked for a better place to be alone with her thoughts.

Well, almost alone. She let herself into Nightwind's stall and held out her hand to greet him. He gently snuffled her fingers, then moved to nibble the pocket of her dress with his soft black lips.

"I'm sorry." Fable sniffed. "No treats today."

Nightwind bumped her arm with his nose, as if to say it was okay.

"At least *you're* not afraid of me."

He nickered gently, and his peaceful presence calmed the last furious shivers of magic within her. She rubbed his nose and thought of how, during her argument with Aunt Moira, it had been swelling and pushing within her like a wild creature.

"Although, maybe you should be."

She squeezed her eyes shut and ran her hands through the pterippus's silky mane. *I need to get control of the darkness inside me! I can't let Endora's bloodline take over.* She swallowed. *If not for my sake, then for everybody else's.*

Why wouldn't her aunt just tell her everything that had happened?

Maybe she's afraid the truth would push me over the edge.

Stop thinking like that, Fable scolded herself. She breathed in the comforting smell of hay and grain. Nightwind's calm emotions folded around her like a comforting quilt. The last of the tension eased from her body.

Nightwind brushed her elbow with his soft lips.

"A lot happened today," Fable told him. "I found a letter my mom wrote to Aunt Moira." Fable's stomach tightened. She'd left the letter and the photo with her aunt. *I hope she gives them back.*

She rubbed her hand down Nightwind's glossy neck. "And we saw Star at the fairgrounds. And then, I came face to face with Orchid!" She paused. "Sort of. I had a surprise astral projection."

She tugged a piece of loose straw from Nightwind's mane and pulled out a knot with her fingers. "Nothing is going right. I thought we'd come here, have a good visit at the Thistle Plum, reunite Thorn and Orchid, have a great time at the festival, get some work started on my house, and then go home to Tulip Manor." *I should have known it wouldn't happen that way. Nothing ever goes as planned.*

Nightwind blew softly through his lips, enjoying the attention from Fable as she continued to comb through his tangled mane. "But tomorrow the festival begins. And then, we can go the games and save Star. And find Orchid. And Sir Reinhard."

It all seemed insurmountable. Why couldn't anything be simple?

The pterippus lowered his head and stretched out his wing. It brushed up against Fable and a feather tickled her cheek. Fable ran her hand over the satiny wing, marvelling over the magic of the creature. In Larkmoor, such an animal was considered a myth. Here in Starfell, while pterippi were rare, they were certainly real.

Fable thought of Moranda, the serpent from the spell list that Moira had insisted was legend. *If pterippi are real, who says sea serpents can't be?*

She stroked his wing and her fingers found a dip in the smooth surface. She frowned and leaned in closer to inspect it. In the consistent pattern of feathers, there was a bare spot. One feather was missing—plucked from its place.

Fable's breath caught. *The spell.* She pulled her book bag in front of her and rummaged through it until she found the wrinkled paper. Nightwind watched her in curiosity as she unfolded it and read, "A feather from a pterippus's left wing."

She was standing on Nightwind's left side. *Endora must have taken it from him that night on Squally Peak!* But she didn't even know about this spell then, did she? *She could have sent somebody here to steal it.*

Fable skimmed to the next line on the list. *Three scales from an uprooter's tail.*

She jammed the list back into her book bag, her

heart hammering, and swung open Nightwind's stall door. He raised his head and nickered questioningly.

"I'm sorry, boy. I have to go." She gave him a quick scratch between his eyes. "I'll come visit again before we leave." She closed the half-door to his stall and paused. "Thanks for the talk."

He gazed at her with liquid brown eyes and bobbed his head, as if he understood.

He does. Fable was sure of it.

She flicked off the light, stepped out into the night air, and ran up the path to the inn. The bright light from her bedroom window let her know that Thorn and Brennus were still up there, probably wondering where she had gone.

She raced up the steps and into the quiet inn. It was late now, and most of the guests would either be in their rooms or out on the town celebrating the start of the festival. Fable strode through the dining room and into the dark, empty kitchen. There, beside the wood stove, sat Piper's plush bed. And sure enough, the fiery lizard lay curled up in it, snoring gently.

Walking softly so she wouldn't scare him, Fable approached the bed. Piper cracked a reptilian eye, then raised his head.

"It's just me." Fable knelt down, the heat from the

stove warm against her side. "Do you mind if I take a look at your tail?"

Piper cocked his head, then stood and turned in a circle and snuggled back down in the soft pillow. He wrapped his tail around the side of his body. Fable lit a glow in the palm of her hand and held it close to his body. The uprooter squinted in the light.

His tail looked just as she'd remembered from the other day—missing several scales, leaving a mottle of grey spots on the normally solid orange appendage.

Endora is gathering ingredients for that horrible spell. She must be. Fable swallowed and sat back on her heels. She wasn't sure if the sweat that formed on her brow was from the heat of the stove or the flame of fear building inside her.

She gave Piper a quick pat on the head and got to her feet. "Thanks, Piper."

The lizard yawned, tucked his nose under his tail, and went back to sleep.

Closing her hand, Fable snuffed out the glow and hurried up the stairs towards her room. Another horrifying thought flashed through her mind, and she missed a step, knocking her shin on it instead. She sat, rubbing her leg, but her tears had nothing to do with the pain.

What about Star and her flock, huddled in that cage

with no use of their only natural defence? They were perfect targets for Endora's vile henchman.

We have to get them out tonight.

She blinked back the moisture in her eyes and got to her feet. There was no time for fear. Star needed her.

Just as she reached the door to her room, Aunt Moira's voice came from the top of the stairs.

"Fable—"

Fable closed her eyes and pushed into the bedroom, pretending she didn't hear her aunt. She couldn't bear to face Aunt Moira again. Not yet. Besides, she had a rescue mission to plan.

SEVENTEEN

Boiling Emotions

Fable stood in the entryway of the Thistle Plum, glaring at the furious Aunt Moira, who stood barring the door. Thorn and Brennus stood to the side, glancing nervously between the two family members.

Fable gripped the edge of her book bag, trying to steady herself. "We have to save Star!"

Aunt Moira puffed out her chest, as if to take up as much space as possible, and gave the teens a hard look. "Absolutely not! She will still be there tomorrow. So help me, Fable, you go back upstairs this instant, or I will cast a barrier around this inn that even Endora with a hoard of her undead couldn't get through."

Fable lifted her chin. "Even if you do set up a barrier, I have the magic to slice through it."

Aunt Moira's face paled with the realization that her niece just might be able to break her magic. She glanced at the cuckoo clock that hung beside the door. "It's past eleven o'clock. Who knows what kind of people are wandering around out there in the dark at this time?"

Brennus piped up. "Probably Doug or Endora's guards. That's the point."

"Trying to steal Star or one of her friends," Thorn added. "For the flame from their last breath."

Fable's stomach clenched and she gave Thorn a panicked look. *Aunt Moira doesn't know that we know about the spell!* She glanced at her aunt, whose eyes were so wide Fable was sure they'd pop from her head. *Well, she didn't know before. Now she definitely does.*

"Where did you get that idea?" Aunt Moira demanded.

Brennus ran his hand through his wavy hair and let out a nervous chuckle. "Well, you see, it started with—"

"What's going on down here?" Fedilmid's sleepy voice floated over them from the bottom of the stairs. He brushed by the children and stood beside Aunt Moira, wearing a fuzzy floor length bathrobe with matching fluffy slippers and a nightcap so long it reached his waist. He rubbed his eyes, then took his rounded spectacles from the front pocket of his robe and placed them on his nose. "You're loud enough to wake an undead from the grave."

"Loud enough to create a new undead, or just wake an undead that's already been raised?" Brennus gave him a weak smile.

Fedilmid pushed his glasses up his nose and peered through them at the boy, a smile tugging at the corner of his mouth. "You know what I meant."

"Timothy has another headache, so I came downstairs to make him a cup of feverfew. I caught them attempting to sneak out." Aunt Moira waved her hand at the teens, then turned to glare at Fable. "After everything we've been through, I thought you'd learned your lesson on reckless behaviour. I thought I could trust you."

A lump formed in Fable's throat. She balled her fists to keep her magic at bay. "You don't understand. Star is in trouble! We saw her today, in a tiny cage with four other firehawks. They could barely move. They were captured for the Magical Menagerie." The words tasted bitter on her tongue.

"They were shackled with magic to stop their fire breath," Brennus added.

"All of the magical creatures in those cages had enchanted chains," Thorn said. "It isn't natural and it isn't right. We need to release them."

Aunt Moira and Fedilmid exchanged worried glances.

Fable gave her aunt a pleading look. "We can't leave her there. She was my first friend in Starfell. If it weren't for her, I never would have gotten to Endora's mansion in time to save Timothy. And I wouldn't have met Thorn and Brennus."

Star had helped Fable when she needed it the most—in a moment even scarier than her confrontations with Endora. She had been Fable's rock in that life-changing moment, when Fable had been torn from Rose Cottage and landed in a strange forest, lost and alone, with no clue about the world outside Larkmoor.

And now, it's my turn to help her.

Aunt Moira brushed aside a lock of stray hair and tucked it behind her ear. "I'm sorry your dear friend is in trouble. But what's one more night? It's not safe to wander the streets in the dark. We can go first thing in the morning to see about her. I promise."

Fedilmid adjusted his night cap, tucking the bobble at the end of it behind his shoulder. "I understand the desire to release Star as soon as possible, but Moira's right. She's most likely sleeping right now. Tomorrow, we can talk to the Menagerie's owner. He may let us purchase her and her friends."

"Purchase her?" Thorn curled her lip. "They're wild creatures. Nobody has the right to own them."

"Of course, but their captor thinks in terms of ownership and money," Fedilmid replied. "Legally purchasing them is our best option to get them out. Then, we can set them free in the Burntwood."

"That could be too late." Fable's heart clenched at the thought of her great-grandmother stealing the firehawks away. She already had Nightwind's feather and Piper's scales, and who knows what other kind of terrible ingredients from the list. Fable was sure that Endora was hunting ingredients, like a cougar stalking its prey in the night. And the component from the firehawk was much more than merely a feather or a scale. It was the flame from a firehawk's *last* breath. That could only mean one thing.

"Endora's looking for her. Now," Thorn said.

Aunt Moira hugged her elbows in front of her, her face drawn. "How do you know that?"

Fable untied the string of her book bag and took out her mother's journal. She opened it to the spot where she had pressed the spell list between the pages, gently lifted the loose paper, and handed it to her aunt. "From this."

Aunt Moira took the paper from her and stared at it with a pinched expression.

"What is it?" Fedilmid peered over the woman's arm. His eyebrows shot up. "Ah. I see."

"It's the missing page from my mother's journal," Fable said.

"Where did you get this?" Aunt Moira gripped the

paper with white knuckles.

"I found it under the cabinet right there, by the door." Fable pointed. "I'm not sure how it got here, but whoever stole it must have dropped it there."

Her aunt's face grew even whiter. The paper crinkled in her trembling hand.

That's when it hit Fable. She gasped, then ripped the spell list from her aunt's fingers.

"Fable!"

"You! It was you all along, wasn't it?" Fable couldn't believe it. First, the secrets about her past and her family, and now this? The one person who was supposed to love and protect her, stealing pages from Faari's journal!

"Fable, you don't think—" Thorn started.

Aunt Moira held up her hand, a pained look on her face.

"It was me. The list must have fallen from my pocket when I hauled the luggage inside." She sucked in a breath and looked at her niece. Her jaw wobbled as she spoke.

"I was cleaning your room shortly after you got back from Endora's mansion and I accidentally knocked Faari's journal off your bed. When it landed on the floor, it was open to the list. I recognized it as something to do with the Blood Star, and I didn't want you to run straight into trouble again. I wanted a safe, normal life. So I held onto it. And then the Blood Star fell and Endora stole it. My fears became true. When we got that letter from Nestor—I knew you would go after Endora again." She gazed at Fable with misty eyes. "It's my job to keep you safe. I can't bear the thought of losing you too."

"I can't believe you!" Magic roared to life in Fable's chest like a fire blazing through her ribs. "It's just like before, with my parents. You ignored Endora and pretended that everything was fine. And you're doing it again! You think if we just carry on as usual that she'll decide to leave us alone. You know how she works. You tried that in Larkmoor and she planted a magical portal right under your nose."

"I'm sorry—"

"No. I can't talk about this anymore. We have a firehawk and her flock to save." Fable folded the spell list, placed it securely inside her mother's journal, and shoved the notebook in her bag. She tied it shut and glared at her aunt.

Aunt Moira straightened her spine, but her face was soft. "We'll talk about this later, once we've all cooled down."

Fedilmid clasped his hands in front of him, his face creased with lines of exhaustion. "For tonight, Algar and I will go to the fairgrounds and check on Star. We can set up a protective barrier around her cage. We are known well enough around town that we won't look suspicious. The rest of you, try to get a good night's sleep. Tomorrow will be a big day." He paused and gave the young teens a questioning look. "Sound like a plan?"

It was better than nothing.

"Yes," Thorn replied for all three of them.

"I'll go wake Algar." The old witch strode to the staircase. He glanced over his shoulder at Fable and her friends. "Star will be okay. Everything will work out in the end."

"All right, children." Aunt Moira's voice was high as if she were fighting back tears. "You heard him. He and Algar will make sure Star is safe for the night. Off to bed."

The trio turned and started up the stairs after the old man.

"Fable," her aunt gave her one last glance. "I am sorry. I should have handled this better."

Fable ignored her and continued to climb the stairs. She was afraid that if she spoke, her magic might do something she'd regret.

EIGHTEEN

Spilled Tea

The next morning, Fable woke early from her restless sleep. She glanced at the bedside clock. *Six o'clock!* She groaned, pushed her blankets aside, and sat up.

Thorn's bed was empty, with only a tangle of blankets where the Folkvar girl had slept. Fable flicked her gaze to the floor beside the armchair where her friend sat cross-legged with her palms on her knees. Thorn's eyes were closed and her braid was a tangle of copper locks pulled this way and that from her restless sleep.

Fable swung her feet to the carpet as quietly as she could. She didn't want to disturb Thorn's meditation. As softly as possible, she crept towards the bathroom.

Just as she reached the door, Thorn opened her moss-green eyes.

Fable stopped, her hand on the doorknob. "Sorry. I didn't mean to bother you."

"It's okay. I just need to settle down before we leave for the fairgrounds."

Fable nodded. The weight of what they might face this morning hung heavy in the air. Star's life was at risk and it was up to them to save her.

Thorn tugged at her messy braid. "Do you think, after we save Star, that we'll have time to look for Orchid? Or at least some clues about where that basement is?"

"Definitely." A prick of guilt pierced Fable's heart. They hadn't even attempted to find the Folkvar girl yesterday. Thorn must be aching inside. "We'll look for her today"

"Thanks." Thorn closed her eyes and settled her hands on her knees once more.

As Fable brushed her teeth, her brain buzzed from the nasty nightmare that had woken her up repeatedly in the night. Despite Alice's herb packets beneath her pillow that were meant for sweet dreams, she'd been terrorized by her own mind well into the wee hours.

She squeezed her eyes closed, trying to rid herself of the dream images. It was no use. Once again, Endora as a decrepit crone with scorched hair and a nasty gleam in her amethyst eyes cackled hysterically, then staggered towards Fable, holding an unconscious Star by her feet. An undead version of Grimm snarled between them, doing his best to protect Fable despite his sagging skin and sad empty eye sockets.

Fable's heart trembled against her ribcage. Magic pooled in her chest, fueled by her heavy emotions. She took a deep breath to banish both the fear and the nightmare images and pushed the wild magic down. *Not now. Not today.*

She spit her toothpaste in the sink, swished her mouth, and quickly changed from her pajamas to her usual knee-length dress—lilac cotton for spring—and black leggings. She grabbed her book bag from the corner post of her bed and went to leave the room.

"Meet you downstairs in a few minutes?" she whispered to the meditating Folkvar with her hand on the doorknob.

Thorn kept her eyes shut. "I won't be long."

Fable closed the door behind her with a click, then padded softly down the stairs to the kitchen.

Alice, wearing a black flannel robe with her long grey hair plaited down her back, sat at the table in the breakfast nook to the side of the cooking area. She was staring into the bottom of her teacup, her face devoid of any emotion.

"Good morning, Alice."

"Oh, Fable." The witch glanced up with glassy eyes. She gestured to a plate of pastries on the island. "Muffins. Juice is in the fridge." Her gaze shot back to her teacup.

"Thank you." Fable gave her a sideways glance. That wasn't like Alice. She was usually bright-eyed and cheerful. *Maybe she's just tired. It's early.*

She took a glass from the cupboard next to the fridge and poured herself some orange juice, grabbed a plate and a cranberry muffin, and joined Alice at the table.

The early morning sun shone through the windows and bathed the nook in soft, warm light. Above them, a bundle of lavender hung from a rod suspended from the ceiling, filling the kitchen with its sweet smell. Despite the comforting atmosphere, Alice continued to stare into the bottom of her teacup with her brows knit together. The longer she looked, the deeper the lines in her face got.

Fable took a sip of her juice, then cleared her throat. "What are you looking at?"

Alice's gaze flicked to Fable's face. She looked surprised, as if she'd forgotten that Fable was in the room.

"The mugwort, dear."

Fable cocked her head. "The mugwort?"

"Yes." Alice jutted a crooked finger at the cup. Her voice grew louder, more insistent. "The mugwort." She titled the cup towards Fable. "Look for the jade antlers."

With a jerk, the old woman stood. She shook the cup in Fable's direction. Soggy tea leaves spilled over its edge.

"Alice!" Fable slid her chair backwards, recoiling from the mess.

"The jade antlers." Alice's gaze bored into Fable with eyes glazed milky blue.

Fable hardly recognized the elderly witch. Her usual friendly demeanor was completely gone, replaced with an air of panic.

"Look for the jade antlers!" Alice shuffled nearer to Fable, keeping one hand on the table for balance.

The jade antlers—that pamphlet in the basement! Maybe Alice knows something.

Fable grasped Alice's arm to steady her. "The jade antlers? What do you mean? Where are they, Alice?"

The kitchen door swung open and Fable whirled in her chair. Nestor shuffled into the room, his face creased with worry.

"Alice, dear." He came and took his wife's hand. "It's okay. You've had another spell. Let's get you to bed."

"Nestor, what's happening to her?"

Alice's agitation pushed against Fable, as if trying to break into her magic. But Nestor radiated calm. *He's seen this before.*

Nestor rubbed Alice's back with his free hand. "It happens sometimes when she's scrying. And lately, she's been doing a lot of it." He shook his head. "Too much. The magic is unstable, and she's growing older. It can be overwhelming even to the strongest witches."

Alice calmed at Nestor's soothing touch. She closed her eyes and set down the teacup.

Nestor continued to rub circles on her back. "Feeling better, dear? You gave me a scare this morning." He glanced at Fable. "I'm usually awake before her so I can get a good look at the stars before sunrise. But this morning when I awoke, she was already out of bed."

Alice's distress eased, but Fable's magic paced inside her as if waiting to pounce on the next bit of emotion flung its way. She clenched and unclenched her fingers, forcing herself to relax.

"Is she okay?" She chewed her lip as she watched Nestor soothe his wife.

He smiled gently. "She will be. She just needs to rest. I dare say we'll have to miss the festival today."

Alice opened her eyes and stared at her hand in Nestor's. "What happened?" Her gaze met Fable's and she let out a small gasp. "Fable! What are you doing down here this early? I . . . I didn't scare you, did I?"

"No, I'm fine. It's you I'm worried about," Fable

214

replied.

Alice took a deep breath. She looked exhausted, and so small and frail. "I'll be fine, dear. I just need to rest."

Nestor took her elbow with his free hand and led her towards the door. "We best get you upstairs, then I'll make you some chamomile tea." He glanced over his shoulder. "Help yourself to anything you like, Fable. There's fresh cut fruit in the fridge."

"Thank you." Fable hesitated. "Um, one thing. Before you go."

"Yes?" Nestor glanced over his shoulder.

"Alice, what did you mean by the jade antlers?"

Alice looked at her and frowned. "Jade antlers?"

"Yes. You told me to look for the jade antlers."

Alice glanced at Nestor, then shook her head as if to clear it from cobwebs. "I'm sorry. I haven't the foggiest idea."

"It's okay." Fable's heart sank. *It has to mean something.* "I hope you feel better soon."

"Thank you, dear."

Alice and Nestor left the room. The door creaked as it swung on its hinges behind them.

The jade antlers. Fable wracked her brain, wondering what Alice could have been talking about. Obviously, it had something to do with Orchid and that basement. Was she supposed to find it? But how?

She glanced at the upturned teacup and the sopping mugwort leaves Alice had dumped on the table. They were useless now.

I have no idea how to scry, anyways.

She stood from the table, got a rag from the sink, and began to clean up the mess. Her magic simmered, stewing like her thoughts. Alice's stilted words echoed in her mind.

Look for the jade antlers.

Just what she needed. One more thing on her to-do list.

She rinsed out the rag and gave the table one last wipe.

The Gift of Unseeing

Fable pushed her book bag out of the way of her jacket pocket and shoved her cold fingers inside. The sun peeked over the horizon with warm rays that held the promise of a beautiful spring day, but the early morning air was still cool and damp. Fresh dew coated the iron bars of the fences that lined the street.

Fable walked between Thorn and Brennus towards the fairgrounds. She glanced at Moira who walked ahead of them with Fedilmid, Algar, and Timothy. The adults chatted amiably as if they were on a normal morning walk to enjoy the sunshine. Fable frowned. Didn't they realize what was at stake if they couldn't rescue Star and her flock? Didn't they care about Fable's friend and the life of misery she'd been literally chained to?

Brennus interrupted her thoughts. "So after we save Star, we need to find Orchid and a set of jade antlers." He tapped his chin. "Easy peasy, right? All in a day's work."

Thorn patted her vest pocket, a determined look on her face. "I don't know about the antlers, but I brought the arrow. I think it could lead us to my sister. It brought Fable to her last night."

"Ssh!" Brennus widened his eyes and jerked his head in the direction of the adults. "We don't want them to know what happened."

His canvas bag hung against his side and his guitar was slung across his back. He'd insisted on bringing it—just in case they needed its magic. At first, Fable had thought he was being dramatic. But when he'd reminded her of the furious whirlwind it created with the *Book of Chaos* on Squally Peak—the tornado that had swept away Endora in a fury of magic—she realized he could have a point.

Thorn rolled her eyes but leaned closer to her friends. "Plus, the arrow led Orchid to us at Tulip Manor, remember?" Thorn whispered. "I think the Collectors are attracted to each other."

Brennus shifted the guitar's strap against his chest and patted his bag. "I brought the astral projection book too. I read more last night, and I'm sure if I tune the guitar correctly, we could make it work properly."

Fable's throat tightened at the thought of going back through the portal. "Let's use that as a last resort. I don't want to risk Aunt Moira seeing us—or being sent to Endora's lair." She shuddered. "Keep an eye out for anything that has to do with jade antlers. That and the arrow are the best clues we have."

Brennus shifted uneasily. "Do you think Alice really saw something in those mugwort leaves?"

The thought of Alice's strange behaviour sent a shiver rolling down Fable's back. "Jade antlers aren't exactly common in Starfell, are they?"

"No."

Thorn cast Brennus a disgruntled look. "Of course she saw something. She's a witch who specializes in divination. And, obviously, whatever she glimpsed in those leaves is tied to Orchid."

They were silent for the rest of the walk to the fairgrounds. Fable's thoughts whirled with images of jade antlers, emerald flames, and cowering firehawks. Her magic swam through her veins, waiting for its chance to strike, to snap out and latch onto the first wayward emotion to cross its path. Fable held her breath for a moment, sending a silent wish universe. *Please, let me be strong. Let me control the darkness inside me.*

The iron arch of the festival grounds jutted through the sun's low rays like the entrance to a gothic fairyland. Aunt Moira led the way through. She glanced at Fable, her mouth tight.

"Where did you say the cages are?"

219

"Beside the games tent." Fable pointed towards the towering red-and-white big top.

The fairgrounds seemed even more mystical today than the day before. Mushrooms and flowers bloomed over moss-covered tents. Dainty lights hung in a criss-cross pattern above the entire carnival. Fable imagined they looked like fireflies at night. She had thought the place would be bustling with preparations for the opening day but it was eerily quiet in the early morning mist.

Brennus ran his hands over the strap of his guitar as they walked. "Jade antlers. It just doesn't make any sense. Antlers are made of bone, not rock."

"I know, but that's what she said—look for the jade antlers." Fable toyed with the tie on her book bag, wondering what kind of animal had antlers made of rock. "And it was written on that pamphlet in the basement. It must mean something."

Thorn slid her hand into her vest and touched the arrow, her brow furrowed. "Divination is weird magic. Nobody knows much about it."

Timothy, who had walked up ahead of the group, turned around and called back to them. "They're empty!"

Fable snapped her head towards him. "What's empty?"

"The cages!"

Ahead of them, the adults crowded around the enclosure where Star and her flock had been the night before. Fable rushed towards them and pushed to the front of the group. Her breath hitched. It was true, the cage was empty. Mottled brown feathers lay scattered in the straw but there was not one firehawk in sight.

In the cage nearest to them, a crimson-eyed wolf with sooty grey fur raised its head and stared at Fable. Its partner with the inky coat continued to snooze, its chest rising and falling in deep breaths.

"How is this possible?" Fedilmid clutched one of the steel bars, staring into the cage in disbelief. "Nobody should have been able to get through that barrier."

"Unless they had strong magic," Algar said gravely, "like Endora does."

"Endora would never come here herself." Aunt Moira's tone was sharp, but the way she wrung her hands together gave away her fear.

Fable's magic battered against her ribs. She tightened her chest, hoping the power wouldn't explode. She wanted to scream. *Where is Star? Did Endora come here and break Fedilmid's shield?*

A piercing whine snatched Fable's attention. The grey wolf pushed its head against the bars of its cage. It studied Fable with scarlet eyes. A mournful voice, drawn out in an eerie howl, sounded in her head.

Cooooome cloooooser . . .

Fable gave the wolf a wary look. "Was that you?"

The wolf winked.

Brennus crouched in front of the door of the fire-hawk cage, inspecting the lock. "It's all melted! Like acid was poured on it."

The giant wolf was now on its feet. It gave a little hop and yipped like a poodle demanding a treat.

Cloooooser . . .

Fable's magic pulled her towards the creature. She inched closer. *What do you want?*

Timothy groaned. "Something doesn't feel right. My head hurts."

Fable couldn't tear her eyes away from the wolf's matted hide and crimson eyes. She took another step towards its enclosure. The creature yelped frantically. Its tongue rolled and saliva frothed around its lips.

"Fable! Don't—" Thorn reached to grab her friend's arm.

But it was too late. Fable took another step forward, avoiding her friend's grasp, and her mind went blank. The world around her went dark. Everybody disappeared, and a mist rolled over the ground. It was almost like stepping through the guitar—but instead of projecting to a new location, it was more like a movie playing in her head. Fable was paralyzed, completely frozen to the spot. She couldn't even move her lips to cry out.

The cages materialized through the mist like props in a stage play, just as they'd appeared yesterday when she'd seen them filled with animals. Behind them loomed the tent like a painted backdrop, the stripes grey in the moonlight. *Wait, moonlight? I must be having a vision!*

The firehawks huddled in the back corner of their enclosure, staring out in horror as two smoky black figures approached.

"'Ere's the wee little birdies." The familiar voice came from the shorter form. It tapped the invisible barrier between them and the frightened birds. A flash of blue rippled out from the spot he touched. "Magic, eh?" It elbowed the stoic lanky figure beside it. "They think that'll stop the likes of us?"

Doug! Fable screamed inside her head, trying to rush forward, but her body wouldn't cooperate. Her eyes bulged as she strained to break free of the bond. She watched in horror as the man cast a green flash over the barrier. It melted away like a light rain sinking into the ground. He poured something over the lock and yanked open the door, then jerked his head at the other figure. It rolled back its sleeve to reveal skeletal arms, then reached into the cage.

Star's high-pitched scream echoed inside Fable's head.

"Fable!"

Fable's body jerked back and forth. Her head wobbled and her eyes flew open. Thorn's concerned face came into focus.

"Pull her away from that mutt." Algar's shout punctured the air. "That's an unseeable. It's entranced her!"

Thorn gripped Fable's shoulders and dragged her away from the yipping canine. Its mate had awoken and joined it. They paced the cage with their hair bristled and teeth snapping, and their howls reverberated between Fable's ears.

Let us ooooouuuuutttt!

Fable stared at the faces around her, trying to get her bearings. Aunt Moira pushed Thorn out of the way and grasped Fable's arms.

"Are you okay?"

Fable blinked. Slowly, the feeling came back into her face and she gulped in a fresh breath of air.

"It was Doug! The wolf showed me."

The horse-sized wolves sat on their haunches, intently watching the group with blazing crimson eyes.

Algar glared at them with his arms crossed, a grizzled woodsman ready to fight. "It's a trick. That's how they lure their prey. You get close enough, they entrance you and show your heart's desire. Then, while you are frozen and distracted, they snap you up."

"Watching Doug and his undead buddy kidnap Star is not my heart's desire." Fable pulled away from her aunt. She glanced at the wolves, meeting the black one's piercing gaze. "It showed me what happened."

Algar's face creased with concern. "They trick people. I've run into them before."

Fedilmid placed a hand on Algar's forearm and looked at Fable. "He's right, they used to hunt in the Lichwood before Endora cleared the forest."

Behind them, Timothy let out a loud whimper. He clutched his temple, his face twisted in pain. "We have to go. Something isn't right."

"We'll get you back to the Thistle Plum right away." Aunt Moira shot Fedilmid a questioning look. "Do you think we should all go—"

"Mom!" Timothy's face turned stark white.

A strong feeling of dread swept over Fable. Her magic sparked, sending a tremor of power up her spine.

A thick roll of brown smog rushed over the ground. Doug appeared behind Aunt Moira as if out of nowhere. Beside him, a bizarre creature in a flowing purple robe with glossy blonde curls lurched into view. It looked like some kind of Goldilocks, but from a twisted tale of horror. When it turned its face towards Fable, the layer of carnivalesque make-up flickered to reveal a skeletal face with gaping holes where its eyes should have been.

Fable's magic blazed through her in a streak of heat and fury. Vibrant green flames pushed at the cuffs of her sleeves.

No! Fable rubbed her wrists together, trying to put out the tendrils of magical fire with her hands.

She was forced to abandon the effort when Thorn grabbed her by the shoulder.

"Run!" Thorn cried.

Fable looked up to see Doug with his arms raised, ready to unleash a torrent of magic against her.

She ran.

Goldilocks and the Emerald Flames

Fable's feet pounded against the pavement, her heart stuck in her throat. She rubbed her hands together, trying to somehow contain her flames and conjure a protective shield at the same time. Pounding along beside her, Brennus shot her a panicked look. Thorn sprinted just ahead of them. Behind them, Fedilmid and Algar ran, Fedilmid shooting bursts of magic over his shoulder. Aunt Moira's skirt flapped in the lead as she pulled Timothy along in a frantic run.

"Mom, wait!" Timothy struggled against her grip. "I think I can—"

"Keep running!" Aunt Moira clutched his arm tighter, her face flushed with fear.

Emerald flames flared from Fable's wrists, swallowing the blue sparks from the barrier she struggled to build. She fought back a sob. *I can't do this.*

She looked over her shoulder in time to see an undead appear from a side alley and step out in front of Fedilmid and Algar. This one wore a bow tie and a crooked top hat. Fable stopped and whirled around.

"Fedilmid!" she called.

"You go on, Fable!" Fedilmid waved his hand to urge her on, then threw another ball of white light at the undead, which it ducked. "Stay with your aunt! We'll take care of this one!"

Fable was about to object, but then the Goldilocks impersonator came at her, Thorn, and Brennus from another alley, and Brennus grabbed her arm and pulled her along. She gulped and looked back over her shoulder to see how close the undead was and noticed a familiar blue whip coiled in its hand. Another undead—or maybe the same one—had used an electrical whip like that to pull Thorn from a wagon last summer like she were a small dog, not a six-foot-five Folkvar. Fable stumbled.

Brennus grabbed her hand and kept her from falling, his eyes wide. "Get your shield thingie up!"

"I'm trying!"

The terror swirled around her like a funnel cloud, gripping and tearing at her magic. Her flames flickered down her arms. She struggled to control the magic, afraid to use it. The fear of what she'd almost done to Grimm crippled her. She'd barely been able to handle the magic she'd been practicing before. Fedilmid had told her to embrace her powers, but what would happen if she embraced these flames? What if she used this fire and it wouldn't be controlled at all?

I can't do it. I'll kill everybody!

Another billow of dirt-brown fog swirled around their feet. There was a flash of movement from the tent alley beside Fable, but before she could call out to warn Aunt Moira, who was several paces ahead of her, the familiar filthy man with the greasy hair stepped out into her path, separating Fable and her friends from her aunt and cousin. Fable skidded to a halt, almost crashing into Thorn.

"Doug!"

Brennus stood beside them, his chest heaving. "Not you again!"

The henchman stood in the middle of the path with a toothpick clenched between his grinning brown teeth. "Fable Nut'atch. Nice t'see yeh again."

Fable scowled, watching him warily. "I can't say the same."

Thorn squared her chest at the man. "Let us by."

Aunt Moira and Timothy whirled to face him.

"Let them go!" Aunt Moira's hair stuck out wildly from her ratty bun, matching the hysterical note in her voice. She raised her hands as though to attack with magic, but Fable wasn't sure what she could do. She'd never seen her aunt do anything but protection spells and barriers. *Does Aunt Moira even have magic that can attack?*

Doug let out a cackle. "Let yeh get away? When Endora will be so happy to see yeh?"

Goldilocks caught up to them and glided to its boss's side, the electric whip still coiled in its bony hand.

Moira jabbed at him with splayed hands, blue light flowing around her fingers. Her voice trembled as she spoke. "I'll turn you into a toad. I will!"

Doug smirked. "I'd like ter see yeh try." He watched her with a smug expression, chewing on his toothpick.

She held her hands in the air for a moment, sweat dripping down her face, then her shoulders slumped and they fell to her sides.

"Tha's wha' I thought." Doug glanced at Goldilocks. "Git the witch and that boy. I'll deal with these brats. I 'as a bone ter pick with them, I do." He snapped the toothpick between his teeth and spat it on the ground.

"Leave them alone!" Fable demanded. But it was too late. The outlandish undead uncoiled its whip and advanced on her aunt and Timothy.

Aunt Moira grabbed Timothy and shoved him behind her, her eyes round as the full moon had been the night before. She rubbed her hands together and began to chant frantically. The undead marched closer, not seeming to notice what she was doing. A blue shimmer flickered in front of the witch, but it winked out in a puff of blue mist.

She's scared. Fable's throat thickened. *She must not be able to channel her magic when she's afraid!*

Timothy stepped out from behind his mother. He marched past her, through the blue mist, and glared at the creature with a fierce look in his eye.

"Stop!"

The undead's feet halted in midstride, as if stuck in a deep layer of mud. Its spine straightened and the whip fell to the ground.

Fable's jaw dropped. *What just happened?*

Suddenly, Doug was upon her, blocking her view of her family. He grabbed her jacket with a gleeful look on his pock-marked face. Fable struggled to wrench free, but she couldn't break the man's grip.

Brown mist formed around the man's hands. He smirked. "Between you all and that firehawk friend o' yers, I'm really gonna make me Mistress's day."

Fury climbed its way up Fable's chest and she thrust her free arm into the air. At that exact moment, Thorn and Brennus jumped on the man. Thorn wrapped her arms around Doug's chest, lifting him off his feet, while Brennus pried his fingers from Fable's sleeve.

Before she could stop it, Fable's magic sprang to life and snatched the dark coil of terror that hovered around her head. Green flames burst from her hands, roaring straight into the vile henchman. Thorn jumped back but Brennus was too slow.

He let out a cry of pain that punctured Fable's heart. The sleeve of his jacket lit up with emerald fire. He waved his arm feverishly in the air, hollering wildly.

Fable's breath shattered inside her ribs. Her heart cleaved in two. *What have I done?* She couldn't move, her body stiff with terror.

Thorn yanked the canvas bag and the guitar from Brennus's shoulder and flung their straps around her neck. In one quick movement, she grabbed the back of his jacket, ripped it from his body, and threw it onto the pavement, then used her hands to put out the few remaining flames on his shirt.

The flame had blasted Doug to the ground, where he lay with his face blackened and clothes aflame. The nearby foliage and tent had also caught fire, and a giant green wall of magical flame stretched across the alley-way. Fable lost sight of her aunt and Timothy on the other side.

"Run, Fable!" Aunt Moira shouted through the flames. "We're fine. You three, run!"

Doug sat up, his eyes dark with rage in his sooty

face. He frantically patted his flaming shirt and shouted at Fable, his face contorted in rage. "I should've known yeh'd fight dirty, bein' Endora's blood an' all!"

Endora's blood. Fable stood rooted to the spot, gaping at the fire. She turned to her friends, her eyes brimming with tears.

"Let's go!" Thorn gripped Brennus's good arm, grabbed Fable's, and pulled them away from the burning henchman, who sent a yell of pain and fury after them.

"Let's go!"

Brennus groaned in pain. He looked up and his eyes widened. He jerked his head to a rickety storage shed a few stalls down. "Jade antlers."

"What?" Thorn squinted at him as if he'd gone crazy.

"Jade antlers!"

Fable craned her neck and saw a set of antlers, the shade of green that matched Thorn's eyes, sticking out through the smog and smoke. They were fastened above the rough wooden door of a crooked shed covered with lichen.

Fable's mind clicked. *Jade antlers, of course!* She'd seen them when she and Timothy had first visited the fairgrounds on Nightwind's back. At the time, with the excitement of the new colours and sights and sounds of the festival grounds, she hadn't thought much of them.

The trio rushed to the shed, leaving Doug stomping on the flames that had surrounded him. Thorn yanked open the door, and Fable and Brennus scuttled inside. With one last glance behind her, she joined them and slammed the door.

Fable's thoughts blurred in a daze. Her magic had retreated after its chaotic burst, and now lay still in the pit of her stomach as if nursing its wounds.

She glanced at Brennus, who held his injured arm to his side. The sleeve of his sweatshirt had melted to his skin in a patch of blackened and charred fabric.

I did that. Horror crept up her spine, one vertebra at a time. She stared at her friend, unable to speak.

"Stop gaping at me and tell us what else Alice said," Brennus snapped at her. "Doug could be here any second!"

The words hit her like a smack in the face. She looked from him to Thorn, her mouth hanging open. "N-nothing! Just 'find the jade antlers.' That's it." She looked back at Brennus. "Your arm—"

"We don't have time for you to heal him yet. We need to get somewhere safe." Thorn heaved a frustrated sigh, then paced the empty shack. Brennus's guitar thumped against her chest. The canvas bag swung from her neck.

Shame washed over Fable. She was secretly relieved to put off healing Brennus's arm. She bit the side of her cheek. *I can't believe I could even think that way.* But it was better than her magic failing and hurting him even more.

"I can take the guitar." Brennus gestured towards Thorn with his good arm.

Thorn pursed her lips. Fable could almost see the wheels turning in her head. Was he strong enough to carry it?

Brennus jutted his jaw. "I can do it!"

Thorn nodded, then helped him strap the instrument to his back.

"What the heck!" Thorn ripped open her vest and pulled out the arrow. It shone so brightly that Fable had to look away. The Folkvar girl eyed the vibrating weapon in her hand. "This thing is going berserk."

"There," Brennus pointed at the ground near the back of the structure, now brightly lit because of the arrow. An uneven layer of dirt met Fable's eye, the lip of a wood board barely visible above the ground. Brennus strode over to it, crouched down, and wiped the dirt away with his uninjured hand.

His face tightened. He adjusted the guitar against his back. "There's no handle."

Thorn marched to the grimy window beside the

door and peeked out. "Doug's almost got the fire on his clothes out. Brennus, get that door open. I'll keep watch. Fable, you help him."

Brennus gave her a curt nod and slid his multi-tool out of his pocket with his good hand. He pressed the button on the side and a flat-edged rod similar to the end of a crowbar popped out. With a quick thrust, he jammed it into the crack between the board and the dirt floor.

Fable's freezing terror thawed, and she knelt next to him. Brennus shifted and tucked his injured arm close to his side, still focused on the job at hand.

I hurt him. One of my best friends in the whole world, and I hurt him. Fable's heart gnawed at her ribs. The fearful look on his face the first time he'd seen her flames snapped into her mind. *He was right to be afraid.*

"Brennus." His name was acrid on her tongue, as if she didn't deserve to say it. "I'm so sorry."

Brennus grunted and wiggled the tool deeper into the crack. The board lifted a few inches. His hand slipped and it bounced back to the earth. "Can you help get this open? When I lift it again, get your hands in there to hold it up. It's not heavy."

Fable swallowed the tears that threatened to spill, feeling like a kicked puppy. *Of course he doesn't want to hear it. Meaningless words from the chaotic girl who'd maimed him.*

"Okay."

Thorn glanced over her shoulder at them, an urgent look on her face. "He's coming. I'm not sure if he saw us come in here, but he's headed this way. Hurry!"

Brennus pushed on the tool again and the board popped up.

Fable shoved her hands beneath it and jiggled until the other end lifted above the ground, then slid it sideways. The stale smell of mould and earth hit her like a bucket of swamp water. Her stomach lurched at the sight of the dank hole beneath the board. Rotting wood stairs with broken steps and loose nails led down into the pitch black. The walls were damp stone with green moss growing in the cracks. A faint dripping echoed from the depths.

Brennus wrinkled his nose and shoved his multi-tool into his back jeans pocket. "Ugh. It's like a crypt. Do we have to go down there?"

Thorn joined them and held Orchid's arrow into the hole, illuminating the first few feet of the crooked stair case. A spider on the second step shrank away from the light and scurried beneath the step.

"Gross," Brennus groaned.

Doug's gravelly voice sounded from outside.

"Come out, come out, wherever yeh are!" He paused, and Fable held her breath. "I'll find yeh, yeh little brats! And when I do, yeh'll be sorry yeh ever attacked ol' Doug."

"We don't have a choice," Thorn hissed. She held the glowing arrow in front of her and stepped cautiously onto the creaky stairs. "Come on."

With a look of disdain into the hatch, Brennus folded his injured arm tightly against his stomach and followed. He tugged at the strap from his guitar, then gripped the back of Thorn's shirt with his good hand. "If these steps break, I'm counting on you to pull me out of the spider's nest under there."

Doug's voice, now raised to a nasty shout, rang out. "I'll find yeh! And then yeh'll have to deal with Endora! And she's not merciful like I am."

Fable, her heart still curled in the furthest corner of her chest, illuminated a glow in her hand and took a shaky step onto the top stair. After she had descended low enough, she gripped the bottom of the hatch cover and pulled it across the opening above her.

The soft thud of the board when it slipped into place comforted her, but it wasn't enough to ease her fear of Doug following them. She glanced below her. Thorn and Brennus descended with cautious steps.

"I'm going to set up a barrier," Fable called down

to them.

"Good idea," Thorn replied.

Brennus peered up at her. "Just don't start a fire down here, okay?"

Fable's heart squeezed tighter into its little ball. She took a deep breath through her nose. *I can't fail them now. Please, let my light shine through the darkness inside me.* She glanced at her friends, who continued their descent.

Don't let me hurt them even more than I already have.

She closed her eyes and started to chant.

TWENTY-ONE

The Bow of Anarchy

The stairs went down for what seemed like forever and lead into a long underground tunnel. Fable's fingers twitched as she and her friends walked through the dark passage. Thorn went first, holding her shining arrow aloft in front of her to guide them. Its soft light glinted off the water dripping from the cracks in the stone walls and pooling on the uneven concrete floor. The pungent smell of mould and damp surrounded them, and their footsteps splashing through the shallow puddles echoed through the space.

Fable checked over her shoulder and listened for the sound of creeping of footsteps. So far, there'd been no sign of Doug following them. Her protective barrier seemed to be holding. Or maybe the henchman hadn't discovered where they went. Either way, they were safe. For now.

Ahead of her, Thorn's arrow flashed vibrant orange.

Thorn frowned at it. "This thing is going crazy.

There has to be something down here."

Brennus glanced at the silky webs draped from the ceiling above them and yanked on the guitar strap across his chest to keep the instrument from brushing against the edges of the passage. "Sure. If you mean spiders, cobwebs, and mildew."

Fable couldn't blame him for being cranky. He hugged his injured arm securely against his stomach. A pang of guilt pierced her.

She was afraid her friends would ask her to heal him. Not because she didn't want to—she desperately wanted to. But she couldn't trust herself to use her magic on him. Not after what she'd already done.

Maybe he won't let me. The thought was strangely horrifying yet comforting at the same time.

Ahead of them, the tunnel jutted sharply to the right, and a heavy wooden door with thick iron hinges and a studded frame could be seen in the corner. An ornate set of antlers, big enough to cover the whole door, had been carved into the wood.

"Jade antlers?" Brennus's eyes grew wide. "Do you think it's safe? What if Endora or her undead are in there?"

Fable shook her head. "If they were, Doug would have found us by now."

"Let's find out." Thorn shoved the arrow into her

vest. It snuffed the light but the arrow glowed through the canvas. She pulled the door open, just a crack, and peered inside the room beyond it.

"I should go first," Brennus whispered. "I'm quieter than you."

Thorn ignored him and pulled the door open wider, filling the chamber with a loud creaking noise. Fable cringed. If somebody was in there, they knew about the trio's presence now.

The Folkvar girl pulled the brightly lit arrow from her vest and held it gingerly between two fingers. "There's nobody in there. But something is shining on that table and this arrow was burning a hole in my shirt."

They stepped into the room and Fable's breath caught. Her hunch had been right. She *had* been here before. Or, at least, her mind had been.

"This is it. The basement from—" Fable broke off when her gaze rested on the brilliantly shining weapon on the table at the end of the room. "Thorn, that's a bow."

The three of them rushed to the table, Thorn leading the way with her massive strides. Sure enough, it was the bow, exactly as Fable remembered it. A leather quiver filled with arrows sat propped against the wall next to the table.

Thorn laid her arrow next to the weapon. Both items shone so brightly that Fable had to shield her eyes. With a gentle wave of golden energy, it seemed like the objects breathed a sigh of relief as if they were two pieces of the same puzzle, finally back together again. Their lights faded to a dull happy glow.

Fable placed a hand on her book bag and, sure enough, it radiated warmth. All of these Collectors were connected. All had been born from Endora's greed and yet somehow had been transformed for good instead of evil.

Brennus stared at the objects, their lights reflected in his warm brown eyes. "Imagine what these could do with the book and the guitar."

Thorn picked up the pamphlet that lay next to the bow and the broken arrow. "Order of the Jade Antlers." She flipped it open, holding it in the dim glow from the Collectors. "The ink is faded, but it looks like a recruitment flyer." She squinted at the paper. "I think this part says 'join us in ridding Starfell of evil.' What does that mean?"

Brennus reached towards the paper with his injured arm. "Ouch!" He winced and immediately hugged his arm back to his side.

"Oh, Brennus." Tears sprang to Fable's eyes. "I'm so sorry."

"It's okay."

"It's not," Fable shot back, her anger directed at herself. "I'm a monster. I hurt Grimm. Almost attacked Malcolm. And now you!"

"It was an accident," Brennus said softly.

"They were all accidents," Thorn added. "You're not a monster. You didn't mean to."

"That's the problem!" Fable balled her fists and held them to her eyes. "I didn't mean to. I didn't want to. But it happened anyways. There's something inside me that's bad. Endora's rage. Her selfishness. Her evil blood. It's inside me and I can't hold it back."

She shrank to the floor on her knees, ignoring the damp cold that seeped through her leggings. A sob escaped her lips. "I've been fighting to hold it in this whole trip. It's been growing since that night at Tulip Manor when I hurt Grimm. Endora—she's part of me. Her dark magic and treachery—it's seething inside me too."

Brennus squatted in front of her and lifted her chin with his good hand, meeting her gaze. "That's not true. You've always been a bit chaotic, but every sorcerer or witch in training is."

Thorn bent down and placed her hand on Fable's back. "He's right. You always fight for good. And that's what matters. You've never let us down."

Fable sniffed. "That's not true. I haven't done good at all. Not lately. Look at today, I barely even helped us get away from Doug and I maimed one of my best friends in the process. Then, I froze inside that shed and couldn't do a thing."

She'd always felt strong with her friends, the one who lead the way and helped them get through the hard stuff. These last few days, when confronted with the things that mattered most, she'd failed. She'd had to rely on Thorn and Brennus to get her out of trouble. To help her get through it all. *If it hadn't been for Thorn's steady leadership and Brennus's guidance*—she swallowed—*we wouldn't be standing here in this basement.*

Brennus rocked back on his heels and raised an eyebrow. "Even if it was a bit out of control, without your flames we would never have gotten away from Doug."

Thorn thumped her back. "Besides, you don't always have to be in charge. Sometimes we have good ideas too. It's okay to rely on us to take the lead once in a while."

Brennus nodded. "Yeah. We're a team. The best team I've ever been a part of."

Thorn smirked. "You mean the only team, right?"

"Don't ruin the moment." Brennus thumped her shoulder gently with a balled fist.

Fable sniffed and rubbed a tear away with her sleeve. Her friends had a point. She couldn't imagine facing Doug or Endora without them.

"Besides," Thorn added. "Does Endora have healing powers like you? If she does, she doesn't use them. That's what makes you different from her. You choose to use your magic for good. That's what makes you, well, you."

Brennus jerked his chin towards his arm. "Now, are you going to heal this, or what?"

Fable gulped. Could she heal him? Should she even try?

"I'll help," Thorn said gently. "You can use my energy."

Brennus nodded. "I'll never forget how you healed Thorn last fall. How you just took hold of my emotions and used them to save her. If that isn't pure goodness, I don't know what is."

Fable still hesitated. "What if I make it worse?"

"You saved my life," Thorn said earnestly. "You can heal a burn. Easy."

Brennus held his arm out to her. Fable's heart warmed. He trusted her. Thorn believed in her. With them, she could do anything.

"Okay." Fable whispered the word so quietly that she wasn't sure if she actually said it out loud. Gingerly, she laid her fingers on Brennus's injured arm. Thorn rested her hand gently on Fable's back.

The melted fabric was rough and hard beneath Fable's fingertips. She closed her eyes and let her taught emotions unspool and flow through her.

I can do this.

She'd never been so afraid as when she'd looked down on Thorn's lifeless body that night on Squally Peak. But, with Brennus's help, she'd brought Thorn back from the brink of death. And now, her friends needed her again. Their friendship and hope wrapped around her like a warm blanket of pure white energy. Her magic reached for the white light and merged with it into a flowing river of love and healing.

Brennus relaxed and let out a breath. "That feels so much better."

Fable opened her eyes. Brennus rolled up the charred sleeve to reveal perfect russet-brown skin. There was no sign of any damage or trauma.

"Wow!" Brennus ran his hand over his healed forearm. "It feels softer than before."

The creak of the door's hinges whined in the air. Muffled footsteps entered the room and abruptly stopped.

"Thorn?" A girl's voice rang out in disbelief.

Fable craned her neck. The lanky Folkvar girl she

met in the basement the day before ducked through the doorway.

"Orchid!" Thorn's voice cracked with longing.

A knight with shining metal armour stepped into the room behind Orchid, his face hidden behind a gleaming visor.

Fable's heart leapt to her throat.

Sir Reinhard!

Folkvar Family Reunion

Sir Reinhard flicked on the light switch next to the door, illuminating the dingy basement. The room was sparsely furnished. A couple of old wooden chairs sat on either side of the table, and a saggy brown couch was tucked kitty-corner to it along the wall. A grimy refrigerator sat along the back wall next to a small kitchenette that looked as though it hadn't been used in years.

Thorn let out a strangled sob. "Orchid! I can't believe it's you."

The sisters rushed across the room and into each other's arms.

"Thorn! I was so scared you were dead." Orchid hugged Thorn's wide shoulders with her slender arms. The two sisters had the same moss-green eyes and matching wild copper hair, but that's where the similarities ended. Thorn's wide frame almost hid Orchid's wiry figure from Fable's view, but Orchid was almost a full head taller than her sister. She even towered over

Sir Reinhard.

Fable's thoughts spun in confusion. *Why is Sir Reinhard here? And how does he know Orchid? Did they meet in Endora's mansion?* That didn't make sense. They would have been imprisoned in separate frames. Fable and her friends had looked for Orchid, but she wasn't there—only Thorn's poor parents had been in that hallway. And Sir Reinhard's portrait had been in her great-grandmother's library, away from the others.

She glanced at the stack of tiny bones that lay on the table next to the bow. Malcolm had been here with Orchid earlier, so he must be friends with Sir Reinhard too. *What does he have to do with all of this? How do these three know each other?*

Thorn's voice was choked with emotion. "I was afraid I'd lost you forever. Up until last fall, when you came to the Lichwood."

Orchid pulled away and regarded Thorn with a serious gaze. "You saw me in the Lichwood?"

"Behind the barrier at Tulip Manor. I've been staying there with Fable and Brennus and the Fey Witch." Thorn's words rushed from her mouth. "I tried to reach you, but Endora's undead chased you away."

Orchid tilted her head to the side, a troubled look on her face. "I don't understand. Tulip Manor? The Fey Witch? I didn't see you or anybody else while we were in the Lichwood. We were on our way to Endora's mansion to rescue more people. My bow sparked with light when I went in a certain direction, almost acting like a beacon of some kind. I tried to follow where the signal was strongest. Are you saying it led me to you?"

"Yes!" Thorn nodded vigorously. "Because of Fable's book. They're connected."

"Fable?"

Thorn waved her hand in Fable and Brennus's direction. "And Brennus. My friends."

"You're the kids who escaped Endora's mansion!" Sir Reinhard strode forward. His metal armor clanged as he walked. He fumbled with the visor of his helmet. It clinked closed and he pushed it up again to reveal his flushed face. "You helped me escape." He rested his gaze on Fable, still holding the visor in place. "Quick thinking on your part. Blasting the glass of my frame, then pushing the lich towards me so I could pull her into it."

Fable smiled. "Quick thinking on your part too, holding her there so I could seal her in." Her throat thickened. "I'm sorry we left you there. I'm so glad you got out too!"

Sir Reinhard grinned and the visor slipped, covering his face. "Of course! It was a bit dicey, what with all those undead around, but I had the power of Estar to help." He pushed the visor back up.

Estar? Fable had never heard that name before.

Brennus scrunched up his nose. "Estar?"

Thorn shifted the canvas strap of Brennus's bag on her shoulder. "Estar isn't real—"

"She is." Orchid countered. "I didn't think so either. But then I met Sir Reinhard."

Thorn blew a breath through her lips. "Wait, what happened to you that night in the Greenwood? And how did you meet Sir Reinhard?"

"And why were you in the Lichwood that night?" Brennus asked.

Thorn's sister and the knight exchanged a glance. His visor clanged shut.

Orchid swatted the air in his direction. "Just take it off."

Sir Reinhard shook his armoured head.

Fable drummed her fingers on the side of her book bag. "Maybe we should start from the beginning."

Orchid closed her eyes. "It's a long story."

"Give us the quick version," Brennus said. "Doug's outside—Endora's henchman."

"We know him," Reinhard said shortly.

Brennus nodded. "Fable set up her barrier in the shed, but if you two got through it . . ."

Fable's ribcage tightened. Did her magic fail again?

"We came through the sporting tent." Sir Reinhard's words were muffled from inside his helmet. "After the tunnel turns, it leads there. This place is secret. I don't think Doug knows about it. We should be safe for now. Take a seat." He gestured towards the saggy couch.

Fable wiped the dust from the seat before she sat gingerly on the edge of it. Brennus leaned his guitar beside the couch and flopped down next to her. Thorn took a seat on one of the wooden chairs. It creaked beneath her weight.

Orchid picked up the broken arrow from the table and twirled it in her fingers, reminding Fable of Thorn. Despite their difference in stature, the similarities between their looks and mannerisms made it easy to see they were sisters.

Orchid paced the room, hugging her elbows. "The night of the forest fire was complete chaos. Mom and Dad were with me. We were running through the burning trees and the flames were scorching hot against our backs." She flicked her gaze to Thorn. "We couldn't find you."

Thorn stared at her sister, her voice barely a whisper. "I fell behind. A tree crashed down between us and I was forced off the trail."

Orchid stared at her sister with misty eyes. "We

didn't know where you'd gone. We tried to look for you, but with the fire—"

"I'm slow. It's not your fault." Thorn swallowed and waved her off. "Then what happened?"

Orchid's mossy eyes grew cloudy. She pressed her lips together. "One of those undead creatures that Endora uses chased us. I tried to shoot it with the bow and then"—she tapped the arrow on her palm—"well, I don't really know what happened. There was a bright flash and suddenly we were surrounded by smoke. It felt like I was falling. And when I opened my eyes, all I could see was that creepy hallway with all the portraits." A tear fell down her cheek and she wiped it away. "Mom and Dad were trapped inside a portrait across from me, pounding on the glass. I was in one too. There was no way to even talk to each other, let alone get out. We tried. Dad had his ax and everything, but nothing worked."

A shudder rolled through Fable's body. Her stomach tensed at the memory of Thorn's parents and their frozen gazes from the portrait in Endora's hallway. And Timothy's face from behind the glass of another, twisted into a scream, his eyes darting to meet hers—

Her magic twitched. A spark like static electricity snapped through her joints. She took a shallow breath, trying to ease her racing heart.

"We saw them," Thorn said. "When we were captured by Endora."

Orchid's chin trembled. "Did they make it out?"

Thorn dropped her gaze to the floor. "No."

Orchid gripped the arrow with white knuckles. The ache in her voice pierced Fable's heart. "I was afraid of that."

"How did you escape?" Thorn asked. "We didn't see you. You must have gotten out before we were taken there."

Orchid glanced at Sir Reinhard, who clumsily lifted the visor of his helmet with a tinny creak. "I smashed the glass of her portrait with my sword."

"Wait," Brennus raised a brow. "When? Weren't you transported into your frame from a Collector?"

"A Collector?" Sir Reinhard frowned. "No, I've never seen one of those. I stormed her mansion to free the souls on her walls. Like Orchid, here. Unfortunately, Endora caught me in the act. The next thing I knew, I was stuck inside that portrait in her library."

"You went there alone?" Fable couldn't believe it. Why would anybody do that?

"And just marched up the front steps?" Brennus raised his palms in front of him. "Are you insane?"

"Most certainly not!" Sir Reinhard motioned to the pamphlet in Thorn's hands. His visor slammed back down over his face, muffling his voice once again. "I have Estar on my side."

Brennus snorted.

Thorn looked at Orchid, her brow furrowed. "Is he serious?"

"Who is Estar?" Fable asked.

Orchid pointed the arrow at Sir Reinhard's head. "Just remove the helmet."

Sir Reinhard's grunt echoed from inside the metal headpiece, then he pulled it from his head. Wavy brown locks flopped over his forehead and ears. Something green poked out from between his curls.

Brennus let out a gasp. Thorn stared at the knight as if a firehawk perched on top of his head. But it wasn't a firehawk. That would have been reasonable compared to the two jade-coloured prongs sticking out from the top of Sir Reinhard's curls. They were only a few inches tall, but they were definitely a young set of antlers.

Thorn stared at him with eyes as round as tennis balls. "'Follow the jade antlers.' Estar is real."

"Would somebody care to explain what's going on?" Fable asked. "Who is Estar? And why do you have antlers on your head?"

"Estar is a powerful celestial peryton." Sir Reinhard tugged at a strand of hair with his free hand and smoothed it around one of the prongs. "And I'm a warlock bonded to her. That's why I have these." He gestured towards the top of his head. "I'm part of the Order of The Jade Antlers. We serve Estar and her mission to stomp out the veins of evil that run through Starfell. Including liches like Endora."

Hope ignited in Fable's chest like the flame of a candle. They had help! *We have a whole order on our side!* "So, there are more of you?"

Sir Reinhard rubbed his chest plate with a gloved hand. "Er, well, there are three of us. Now that Orchid has joined."

"Three people? That's it? How is that an order?" Brennus asked.

The knight narrowed his eyes at Brennus. "There aren't many warlocks left. And most are living beyond the edge of Starfell in the Oakrath Thicket, a dead gloomy place, looking for a way in." He paused. "After some rogue warlocks tried to storm the Ministry here in Mistford—well, they disappeared and the rest of us were all banned from Starfell. Estar is the only patron who has managed to get a warlock back inside. That's why I had to recruit Malcolm for help."

Fable snapped her fingers. "Of course! I saw Malcolm here with Orchid when I projected here."

Sir Reinhard nodded. "I found him in Stonebarrow and convinced him to join me. A necromancer proves quite helpful against undead soldiers like Endora's."

Brennus's face paled. "He's a necromancer?"

"No wonder he has all those weird bones and skins." Thorn shuddered.

Fable's stomach clenched at the memory of Malcolm's interest in Timothy at the Thistle Plum, followed by the image of the undead earlier today—frozen mid-pace at her cousin's command. "What's a necromancer?"

"He can raise and control the dead," Sir Reinhard said. "They're very rare."

Control the dead? Every day, more mysteries and strange magic popped up around Fable. Why couldn't Aunt Moira have taught her and Timothy anything about the real world of Starfell? Why did she have to shuttle them away to Larkmoor, hidden from the truth about magic?

"Can Malcolm control Endora's guards?" she asked.

"To a certain extent," Orchid replied. "He can control them when Endora isn't around. But if she's close, her pull is too strong. They only obey her when she's near."

So Endora wasn't at the grounds herself, then.

"Is Endora a necromancer, too?"

"Liches have some bone magic," said Sir Reinhard,

his face grave. "But they have to be within several feet of the bodies they choose to raise. A necromancer's reach is much longer."

"And the dead she brings back are mere shells of themselves," Orchid added. "A necromancer can bring back a being's mind. It's a twisted version of life, but somebody who's been raised by a necromancer is capable of thought and independence. Not like one of Endora's undead."

Fable thought back to the bizarre undead with the golden curls halting at her cousin's command. *But Timothy—it's impossible. How could he be a necromancer? He's never had magic.* Did he even know what he'd done?

The room was silent for a few moments as Fable and the others considered the extent of Endora's evil. Fable's magic shifted inside her as if uneasy at the thoughts racing through her mind. *Is that what I'm fighting inside me, too? Power that can raise the shell of a dead body with no respect for the person it once was? How will I ever stop a bloodline that is so vicious?*

Brennus pointed at Sir Reinhard's head. "What are you going to do when those grow as big as a stag's?"

"I haven't thought that far ahead yet." Sir Reinhard's cheeks reddened and he darted his glance to Orchid. "We'll figure out something, though."

"Why do you have antlers in the first place?" Fable asked. None of this made any sense. *Aren't warlocks evil?* Why would he free Endora's captives?

"Warlocks adopt traits from their patrons," Brennus said. "I read about it at Tulip Manor. As the power from their sponsor seeps into them, so do certain physical attributes. It's an unavoidable side effect."

Sir Reinhard gave him an impressed look. "That's right. And while these antlers aren't ideal, they aren't quite as bad as what some other warlocks have to deal with."

Brennus glanced at Fable and Thorn. "Remember what my parents told us Ralazar looked like?"

Sir Reinhard's head jerked up. "Ralazar?"

Fable nodded, remembering Isla Tanager's hushed voice when she spoke about her and her husband's captor.

"He had red scaly skin and reptilian eyes."

Thorn swallowed. "Halite. He's bonded to the queen of dragons."

"Correct." Sir Reinhard cleared his throat and gave Brennus a nervous glance. "Is Ralazar here?"

"I don't know. He trapped my parents in his Odd and Unusual Store. It teleports all around Starfell. It has a spot beside the Drippity Cone here in Mistford.

That's how we found them last fall," Brennus replied. "But we didn't see Ralazar here. Only my parents."

"He released them from Endora's wall," Thorn said.

"He what?" Sir Reinhard's face went pale.

"With magic, not a sword." Brennus straightened and gave Sir Reinhard a hard look. "Fedilmid told me that warlocks trick people into helping them. Ralazar cursed my parents into slavery. Who's to say you're not doing that to Orchid and Malcolm? Or trying to do that to us?"

Sir Reinhard held his helmet in front of him, his face sober. "I'm not evil. Or tricky. Nor is my patron. She's celestial. She's good."

"I'm not bound to him by magic," Orchid added. "He helped me escape with no strings attached. I chose to stay with him when he found me again in the Lichwood after he escaped Endora. I want to help rid Starfell of evil like her."

Fable glanced at Brennus. "He helped us get away from Endora without expecting us to repay him. I don't think he's like Ralazar."

Orchid held the palm of her hand to her head. "How did Ralazar get back into Starfell?"

"We don't know," Brennus replied. "All we know is that he had some sort of deal go bad with Endora, and, out of spite, he took my parents."

Sir Reinhard rubbed his left prong, a worried look on his face. "So Starfell has more problems brewing than merely Endora."

Fable's magic sputtered inside her. *Merely Endora!* "You do know what she's capable of, don't you?"

Sir Reinhard's face flushed. "Of course we do, but—"

The door to the room swung open and Malcolm raced inside. He slammed it behind him. His face was a sickly green, his eyes wide with panic.

"Endora!"

Fable's magic slammed into her stomach. She jumped to her feet just as the room filled with foul brown smog. It was so thick she couldn't even see Brennus on the couch beside her.

No!

Her great-grandmother's evil cackle filled the room. Icy fingers gripped Fable's forearms in a sharp grasp. Before she could react, the fog compressed around her.

A bright orange light appeared in the thick haze, and Fable gasped. Orchid's glowing arrow shot towards her, and then the brown fog enclosed her completely.

The Bottomless Sea

S alty air rushed into Fable's lungs. She opened her eyes to a velvet sky scattered with glinting stars. Wet sand shifted beneath her fingers as she pushed herself up to sit.

Where am I? What just happened?

Endora's evil cackle filled the air, and she remembered the smothering brown fog in the basement. *Endora kidnapped me!* A wave of terror crashed through her, and her magic roiled inside her in a frenzy of emotion, gnashing its teeth like a caged wolf.

She jumped to her feet. Beside her, Malcolm stood rigid, as if ready to bolt. His spindly fingers gripped a small bone, yellow with age, which was slender and curved and looked like some type of animal rib. He whispered frantically under his breath and darted his gaze around the beach, searching for the assailant who had torn them from Mistford.

The sand stretched for miles in either direction, with a thick forest on one side and the gentle waves from the ocean lapping on the other. It was the blackest sea Fable had ever seen, even in pictures from their textbooks at her school in Larkmoor. A ripple of movement in the shallows broke the glassy surface.

Fable swallowed. *This must be the Bottomless Sea.*

A woman who could only be Endora stood near the waves, her back to Fable and Malcolm. Her ebony hair was swept into a twist, showing off the back of her ankle-length sequined black dress. Doug stood next to her. A mist of putrid smog dissipated into the air around them.

The lich glanced over her shoulder. Fable's heart thumped in her chest. The last time she'd seen the woman, she'd been weakened and old—being separated from her mansion and the lifeforce stored within it had caught up with her. Now, she was as young and beautiful as ever, with smooth creamy skin and sleek ebony hair. Clearly, she'd nursed her wounds and healed over the winter. Fable cringed, thinking about the souls the lich must have consumed.

A tendril of angry magic wound its way from Fable's stomach into her throat, emboldened by the fear inside her. She clenched her jaw, hoping to push it down—to keep control before she did anything to make the situation worse.

Endora's blood-red lips curled into a cruel smile.

"Fable. So nice to see again."

She turned to face her great-granddaughter, one of Orchid's arrows clutched in her claw-like hand. "Wretched Folkvar." She snapped the arrow in half, tossed it to the ground, then gestured towards a tear in the long sleeve of her dress. "My dress is ruined! Does she have any idea how expensive this was?" She smirked. "Of course she doesn't. Filthy woodsfolk have no concept of money. Or class. I thought I put her down for good last time."

Fable lifted her chin, her magic sparked to attention at the mention of Thorn. "She's stronger than you think."

"Was it her strength?" Endora smirked. "Or was it you that saved her? Using the power you got from me."

"You gave me nothing." Fable wished she believed the words. But the swirling mass of dark energy inside her begged to differ.

Malcolm stood rooted to the spot next to her, clenching the rib bone. He stared at Endora, looking like a cornered cat, his eyes wary and face drawn. He was still muttering under his breath, the bone still in his hand.

"I don't think so, necromancer," Endora hissed.

She raised her arms and a blast of crimson hit Malcolm's chest. The rib fell from his fingers and disappeared into the sand below him. His body stiffened and his eyes bulged. He fell to the ground with a soft thump.

Fable's pulse throbbed as she bolted to his side. "Malcolm!"

He flicked his gaze to hers, but didn't move.

She spun to face the lich. "What did you do to him?"

Endora narrowed her eyes at Fable. She gestured towards the man with her long nails. "Don't fret, child. He's merely having a nap for now. Until I need him."

"For what?"

"You'll find out soon enough."

Another ripple in the dark shallows of the water caught Fable's eye. "You're gathering ingredients for the Blood Curse, aren't you? I know you have Nightwind's feather and Piper's scales." She stuffed down her fear, thinking of her firehawk friend. "Where's Star?"

Endora tilted her head. Her dangly diamond earring brushed her shoulder. "The Blood Star?" She let out a piercing laugh. "Do you honestly think I'd tell you where I've hidden it?"

Fable's magic slammed against her ribs, feeding off the anger that boiled inside her stomach. It was all she could do to keep it from exploding from her chest.

I need to keep my head. Endora's smart. If I lose control, she'll easily overtake me.

"I meant the firehawk. And her flock."

Endora titled her chin with a haughty laugh. "Why would I want such a dirty little creature? I don't have any fire-breathing chickens."

Doug's mouth flopped open in protest. "I got'em! They's at yer mans—"

"Shut your mouth, you fool!" Endora whirled on him, her teeth bared like a rabid hound.

Doug scowled and crossed his arms. "Yeh don't have ter yell at me."

Fable's heart shattered. Her magic froze, as if unsure of what to do with heartbreak and sorrow. A tear formed in her eye. *She has them.* Star and her friends, they were inside that hideous palace of death and gloom—the house that swallowed innocent souls and fed them to an evil lich.

Endora, her attention still on Doug, clenched her teeth in a vicious snarl. "You haven't got everything yet, have you? Go back and finish your job. Or a portrait will be waiting for you on my wall."

Doug stumbled backwards. He shook out his wrists and brown fog poured from the cuffs of his sleeves. "Jeez. I thought yeh'd be happy I found the brat. And a necromancer. Ma'am."

"What did I tell you about calling me Ma'am?" Endora marched towards him, but it was too late—the filthy man vanished in a cloud of smog.

The magic inside Fable jerked. The portal-caster, her only hope at getting away from this beach and her evil great-grandmother, was gone. And he was on his way to capture more innocent creatures for the Blood Curse.

Fable pushed her power down, then took a step towards Endora, her eyes narrowed. "Is this worth it?"

Endora placed a hand on her hip. "Excuse me?"

"Is this worth it?" Fable repeated, louder this time. "All these souls you're hurting. The innocent creatures and people you're using to—what? Remain young forever?"

Endora marched towards her, her scarlet lips pulled back in a fierce snarl. "You don't know what you're talking about. The Blood Star's magic is owed to me, not some pathetic little imitation like you." She paused, then lowered her voice. "You have no idea what I've lost and will never regain."

Shards of anger tore through Fable like broken glass. "What? Your family? The grandsons you murdered?"

Endora's eyes widened in surprise.

The flames inside Fable roared to the surface,

sweeping down her arms. "I feel your darkness grow-ing inside me but I won't let it out. No matter what spell you use with the Blood Star, I'll never let you use my magic."

Endora's jaw trembled, then she clenched her teeth and grabbed Fable's fiery wrist.

"How dare you!"

A jolt of electricity shot through Fable from her great-grandmother's touch. Her body stiffened, bound in the invisible grip of an icy claw. The emerald flames receded, her magic retreating to the pit of her stomach like an injured animal to its den.

She stood frozen, gaping at her great-grandmother, her legs refusing her command to move. Her tongue was fixed in her mouth, unable to let loose the scream that begged to escape her lips.

The vile lich grabbed the collar of Fable's jacket and yanked her face-to-face. Fable struggled to turn her head away but her neck refused to obey.

"You think my power lives inside you, that my blood has passed to you?" Endora gritted her teeth and twisted Fable's collar tighter. "You think you deserve my magic? You are nothing. I lost my heir years ago. You dare to compare yourself to him?"

Who is she talking about? What heir?

"I lost the successor to my power. The perfect

child." Tears glistened in the lich's amethyst eyes. "Once, I thought you could replace him. But you've proven yourself too weak. Too stupid to accept the gift of power only my bloodline can give." Endora's face twisted and she lifted Fable by the collar of her dress with a white-knuckled fist. Deep lines formed around her eyes and mouth. A streak of grey swept through her ebony hair.

Who is she talking about? My father? Or Thomas? But she murdered them! Fable struggled to kick free of the binding spell. Her magic surged within her but couldn't reach her fingers. Sweat poured down her face, but it was no use. She couldn't break free.

"Your blood is only good for one thing." Endora growled. "For the curse to break the Blood Star free of its path to only serve the light."

She dropped Fable to the ground.

The impact reverberated so hard through Fable's body that she was afraid she was going to shatter. Panic pooled in her chest. Lying on her side with half of her face buried in the sand, she watched in horror as Endora stalked over to Malcolm. The lich hobbled like a crone again. Her pace had slowed, and there was a hitch in her step and a hunch to her shoulders. Her greying hair escaped its twist and hung in ratty locks down her back.

She snapped her crooked fingers and Malcolm's rigid body jerked in the sand, then rose shakily into the air like a puppet on strings. Endora's pruney lips warped into a revolting grin. She staggered towards the edge of the black sea with Malcolm floating behind her.

"You are just the icing on the cake, dear great-grand-daughter." Endora's voice rasped like the sound of fingers scraping on a chalkboard. She stood in the black water up to her knees, Malcolm floating in the air beside her. "This is who I really need for the spell. A conduit who can actually raise the dead, not just empty shells of bones and sinew. Somebody with real bone magic." With another snap of her fingers, the necromancer plummeted into the shallows.

Thrashing and sputtering, he got to his feet and faced the lich. But before he could react, she pulled her dagger from her pocket, snatched his wrist with her other hand, and sliced the blade across his palm. He cried out in pain as she plunged his hand into the water.

A brilliant flash of green light shot from his hand and out to sea, disappearing into the depths. Wind howled over them. Foamy waves crashed above their waists.

"Moranda!" Endora's ragged voice echoed across the waves. "Rise, you foul beast. It's time to fulfill your true destiny!" The wind whipped her tangled locks around her deranged face.

Where the bright light glowed in the water on the horizon, a looming dark shadow appeared and approached the shore more quickly than Fable would have thought possible. It had to be the size of a ship, or even larger. A scaly black nose broke the surface, followed by fiery orange eyes. It hesitated, staring at the lich, who cackled before it.

Fable's heart shrank to the furthest corner of her ribcage. *Moranda!*

The serpent reared from the water, as high as the clock tower in Mistford. Her body, as thick as a redwood tree, glistened in the darkness. Her jaw snapped open to reveal stark white fangs, and an eerie shriek erupted from the depths of her throat.

Fable's magic flooded into her chest, searching for her fear, demanding release. As it pulsed and crackled within her, she only had one thought.

We're all going to die.

TWENTY-FOUR

The Blood Star

Fable gritted her teeth. It was a slight gesture but the only movement she could muster. She tried to cry out to Malcolm, but the invisible claw squeezed her jaw. Panicked magic roared through her, swelling and pressing, looking for any way out. It was as if the spell held her power inside her, trapping it against its will.

Is this what happened to Star when that chain was put around her neck?

And Doug was hunting down more creatures for the curse. *I can't just lay here. I have to break this spell and defeat Endora. For Star!*

At the thought of her friend, a flame of white heat ignited in her ribs in the centre of the chaotic magic that writhed inside her. But this energy felt different. Instead of mayhem and whirling emotion, it flickered warmly like a lighthouse guiding her home. Fable's jaw relaxed. She pushed her magic towards the light.

A piercing shriek filled the air. Fable cut her gaze to the churning dark water. Moranda loomed in the mist and struck at Endora with fangs longer than Fable's arm, but Endora dodged away at the last second. A hysterical laugh escaped the woman's lips as she splashed through the shallows, taunting the creature. Her hair hung in knotted wet tresses around her shoulders. Black mascara ran down her cheeks and her lipstick smeared across her face, making her look like a melting clown.

The evil woman threw back her head to laugh again. Lightning crashed down from the dark sky, illuminating the roiling clouds that formed above them. It hit Endora and, for a fraction of a second, Fable thought she must be dead. But the old crone held her ground. She pulled her hands apart and a crimson bolt of lightning formed between her palms.

Fable's eyes bulged in their sockets.

She caught it! She caught a lightning bolt!

Like the binding spell that held Fable tight, this was new magic. She'd never seen Endora use this type of raw power before. Slashing through the air, the crimson bolt struck the serpent's narrow snout over and over. And somehow, no matter how many times the creature darted and gnashed its razer-sharp teeth, Endora never got hit. She always managed to dart aside at the last second, guessing its every move in a savage ballroom dance.

Malcolm appeared at Fable's side, sopping wet, with a wild look in his eye. His cold fingers grasped her arm, sending an icy shiver through her motionless body. He murmured an incantation under his breath.

The light inside Fable flared, flashing through her. She tried to grip onto it with her magic, but it faltered. The power inside her craved chaos and mayhem, not warmth and light. *Just like Endora.*

But Fable's neck loosened and her muscles re-laxed. While she still couldn't wiggle her fingers or kick her feet, she was able to crane her head to stare at Malcolm. "How did you do that?"

Malcolm patted her legs frantically, as if trying to wake them up. "B-bone magic is a warped v-v-version of healing. Sometimes it can b-break a bond. It wo-won't last long." He paused and cast an anxious glance at the warring souls in the waves. "Come on! We h-h-have to run!"

A flash of crimson lit the sky. A battle cry from Endora cut through the air.

"I can't get up!" Fable bit her tongue, trying with all her might to push her power past the bonds that held her. She looked at Malcolm. "Endora is going to kill Moranda. Send her back into the sea! Can't you control her?"

Malcolm's face paled and he glanced at the beach. "She—she's not d-dead."

"What? Then why did Endora need you?"

"Moranda was th-thought to be dead, but I-I think she was m-m-merely hibernating. I felt her life force when En-Endora f-forced my magic."

The sky flashed red and the serpent wailed again. Through the wind and crashing waves, Fable could only catch glimpses of her writhing body when Endora struck with her lightning. The creature had slowed, weakening her attack against the lich.

Flee! Fable urged the serpent on in her mind. *Get out of here before Endora murders you too!*

Malcolm patted her legs harder, murmuring his incantation under his breath. "I wish I hadn't l-lost my charm. Can you use your h-h-healing powers?"

Fable furrowed her brow and pushed her storming magic into her legs. She'd never tried to heal herself before. It was always somebody else—an injured friend, a wilting plant, or an unconscious dog. Her heart shrank against her ribs. She had no idea how to do this.

I'm too weak. I have darkness taking over inside me and I can't fight it. I'll never be able to heal myself or anybody else ever again. She tried to wipe the tear that ran down her cheek but her hands wouldn't obey.

Out of the corner of her eye, a purple light flickered so quickly that Fable thought she must have imagined it. She twisted her head to look in the direction it came from but only shadows met her eye.

A piercing scream echoed across the beach, followed by a roaring crash as Moranda's body hit the water. Waves as high as Fable was tall crashed to the shore, then trickled down to a gentle swell. The sea had gone black, with no sign of flashing magic or battle-torn creatures.

Fable and Malcolm both froze, watching in horror as Endora's dark form staggered from the water. She collapsed to her knees on the beach, clutching a broken and bloody fang the size of a small dog. Her body hunched over, crooked and warped with age and exhaustion. She fell to the sand with a soft thud, cradling the splintered tooth to her chest as if it were a precious baby.

Moranda's dead. Endora has the fang! Fable let out a strangled sob.

"Fable, h-hurry!" Malcolm seized her arm, sending a jolt into the rapidly dimming light inside her.

A bright flash of amethyst light erupted beside them. Brennus's and Thorn's blurry forms crouched in the glow, blinking and looking around as if lost.

Fable's mouth gaped open.

"Fable?" Thorn frowned, looking at the shore where Endora knelt with the fang.

"Thorn? Brennus? How . . . ?" The light inside Fable bloomed, filling her chest with warmth and hope.

"Fable!" Brennus met her gaze, his face alight with excitement. "We did it! Orchid shot the arrow into Doug's portal. Combined with the bow's powers, it helped guide the guitar's magic to you." He paused, taking in his friend's frozen state. "Wait, what happened to you? What's going on?"

"Endora cast a b-binding spell on her," Malcolm said. "We need to b-b-break it now!"

Thorn furrowed her brow, then tried to place her hand on Fable's shoulder. It went right through her, as if Thorn were a ghost.

"You're just a projection," Fable said. "You can't help me."

Brennus cast an anxious glance in the direction of the crumpled heap that was Endora. "Use your healing. Quick!"

"I can't! I'm too weak. Endora's darkness has taken over my light. I can't do this." A sob escaped Fable's lips.

"Yes, you can." Brennus urged her. "Remember our talk back in the basement? We're a team!"

"Listen to us—" Thorn started, interrupted by Malcolm's squeak.

Endora appeared above Fable, a maniacal grin on her make-up smeared face. She clutched the bloody fang in her hand.

"Use your magic!" Thorn shouted. "Light is stronger than darkness. Remember what Fedilmid said? Embrace your light!"

"Wherever there is light, darkness flees!" Brennus yelled.

Endora faltered, looking at them in confusion. "Where did you come from?" Her face hardened and she slashed through the purple light with the fang.

No! Not my friends! The light inside Fable flared and her magic swept it up like a fish in a stream. Malcolm jumped back from her as if her magic had shocked him. Sweat poured down his pale face.

But nothing happened to her friends. The weapon had gone straight through the light. Fable's friends glared at the lich.

"You can't hurt us," Brennus spat.

"And you can't hurt Fable either!" Thorn agreed.

"Watch me." Endora cackled again and tossed the fang to the ground. She pulled her dagger, still covered in Malcolm's blood, from her pocket and stalked back to Fable. "All I need is a piece of her. A strand of hair. An eyelash. A fingernail. But you know, I think I'd rather take her blood. Blood always makes a curse stronger. Don't you think, necromancer?"

"Endora, n-n-no!" Malcolm stood over Fable to block the lich.

"Oh, get lost." She waved her wrinkled hand at him lazily.

His eyes bulged, his body stiffened, and he fell to the sand beside Fable—bound again.

Fable's heart pounded and the magic inside her swirled. White hot rage mingled with her light. *No!* She tried to cling to the light, willing it to overpower the darkness inside.

Brennus and Thorn rushed the old woman, punching and kicking fruitlessly at her. Thorn tried to wrap her arms around the woman's waist to no avail. Brennus's fist went right through her jaw.

"What do we do?" He cried out with panic in his eyes.

Endora knelt beside Fable, who lay helpless on the sand. The lich turned the dagger in her hand, admiring it in the purple light. She leaned over Fable and something rough and heavy thudded onto Fable's neck. It warmed at the touch of her skin. Fable craned her head to see what it was. A glint of gold shimmer in black stone caught her eye, some kind of pendant attached to a gold chain around Endora's neck.

Is that—could she be that stupid?

The battle-weathered hag lowered her lips and whispered in Fable's ear. "You're nothing. The star is mine. You saw the way it came to my call. It wanted to come home. Back to its mother."

Its mother? What?

The chunk of glistening rock seared against Fable's neck. She wanted to reach up and snatch the Blood Star from the lich's neck, but she still couldn't move. Anger and sorrow writhed within her. This horrible woman had taken everything from her. Her home, her family, her safety, and now Star. She'd never stop until Fable's life was completely destroyed.

Fedilmid's calm voice floated into her head. *You'll never be able to embrace your own magic if you avoid your not-so-pleasant emotions.*

Fable was done avoiding them. Forever.

She took a deep breath and closed her eyes, letting her emotions flow freely for the first time in months. At first, her magic raged, out of control with wild abandon. But the star on her neck warmed, and her magic swelled through her entire body, letting the white light inside her shine through.

At that moment, the bond that held her broke. She'd broken it.

"Fable!" Thorn cried out. "Get up!"

"She's too weak." Endora smirked and straightened, dragging the now-glowing Blood Star with her so it dangled over the collar of her torn dress. Her knotted tresses dripped water onto Fable's cheek. She ran the blade over Fable's hair.

Thorn and Brennus jumped on top of her.

Time seemed to slow. As her friends flew into action, her mind filled with sweet memories of her friends singing in the Lichwood, laughing around the campfire, and trying all the crazy ice cream flavours at the Drippity Cone. Thorn dragging her into the Mistford library after her first meeting with Doug. Brennus strumming his guitar outside Endora's tent on Squally Peak.

"No."

Fable embraced every feeling inside her. The rage,

her love for her friends, the sorrow over her parents and Star.

Fable grasped the lich's wrist. Endora's face barely registered her surprise before Fable sat up and squeezed until Endora dropped the blade.

Fable's white light mingled with the magic roiling inside her like a hurricane, feeding off the emotions that swirled inside her. "You won't ruin any more of my life. It's not yours to play with. I'm not a part of your sick game."

She snatched the star from Endora's chest, breaking the chain that held it in place. Before Endora could react, Fable shoved it in her skirt pocket.

Endora followed Fable's actions with wild, bloodshot eyes. She grasped at the broken necklace, as if she couldn't believe Fable had actually stolen it.

"You horrid little heathen!" The panicked hag raised her arms in front of her wrinkled face. A burst of sparking crimson power flew from her towards Fable.

"NO!" All three of the friends shouted at once, their voices filled with force and determination.

White magic poured from Fable's chest and swallowed Endora's scarlet hatred. It surrounded the lich, illuminating her bony face and sunken eyes. She howled with rage but Fable held on, pouring every ounce of herself into her magic.

Suddenly, the white light winked out. All grew still and silent.

They fell into darkness. Even Thorn and Brennus's purple light had dimmed. But their forms were still there, sitting beside Fable like softly glowing amethyst ghosts. The Blood Star lay warm against her hip. The only sounds were the gentle waves lapping against the sand, and Malcolm's moaning as he rubbed his head and sat up.

Where Endora had sat on the sand moments ago, there was only an empty divot.

The wicked lich was gone.

TWENTY-FIVE

The Stone Stable

Fable ran a wooden comb through Nightwind's silky mane and breathed in the comforting smell of fresh hay and sawdust. It had been two days since the pterippus brought her and Malcolm home from the battle with Endora on the beach of the Bottomless Sea. She finally had the energy to leave the Thistle Plum's safe walls, but she hadn't gone far. The comfort of the stone stable had called to her, and she'd promised Nightwind another visit.

"It sounds like we might be staying here for a while," Fable said to the pterippus.

He sighed in reply, then shifted his weight and relaxed a back leg the way horses did when they were half-asleep.

"Aunt Moira doesn't think the Lichwood is safe anymore. Not sure why she thinks Mistford is any better."

Her aunt's reasoning had been because there were police in the city. Fable was sure Trueforce would keep avoiding the residents of the Thistle Plum. But Aunt Moira was stubborn, and Fable knew she would keep harassing the sergeant until she was heard.

"At least she's given me a few more days off school."

"Speaking of Mom." Timothy's freckled face popped over the half-door. "She sent me here to check on you."

He'd slipped into the barn so quietly that Fable hadn't even heard him. Or maybe she'd been too consumed in her thoughts.

"I'm fine. Nightwind here is taking good care of me."

"I knew he would be." Timothy reached his hand into the stall and let Nightwind snuffle his palm. "Sorry Mom's being such a giant pain. Again. She's just worried about you."

Fable sighed. "I guess I can see why."

Since her and Malcolm's rescue from the beach, made possible by Thorn and Brennus rushing back to the Thistle Plum to tell the adults what happened, she'd been exhausted. She'd expended every ounce of magic within her to defeat the lich. What was left of it slept inside her, recuperating like a battle-worn dragon.

She wondered how Malcolm was doing. Since they'd returned to the Thistle Plum, he'd remained hidden in his room.

He's probably as exhausted as I am. She would never forget the way the necromancer stood up to her terrifying great-grandmother. He could have easily fled to save himself—but he hadn't.

Speaking of necromancers . . .

Fable caught her cousin's eye. "I saw what you did at the fairgrounds."

Timothy's jaw tightened. "What?"

"That was really brave."

Timothy stared at her for a moment, his fingers gripping the top of the stall door. He darted his gaze to the floor. "I don't know how I did it."

"You should talk to Malcolm about it," Fable suggested. "He'll be able to help you figure it out."

Her cousin regarded her with a serious expression, as if he were weighing her words with caution. "Thanks." He turned to leave, then shot one last glance over his shoulder. "Don't tell Mom. She thinks she hallucinated because of how scared she was."

A grin tugged at the corners of Fable's mouth. "Of course she does. I promise I won't tell her anything. It's up to you, when you're ready."

"Thanks."

Right after he left, the door slid open again and Thorn and Brennus entered the stable.

"Hey, you," Brennus said.

"Do you feel up for some yoga?" Thorn asked. "Alice said she'd finally give it a try. She's waiting in the backyard."

Brennus leaned his elbows on the top of the half-door of the stall. "I even mowed so we won't have to battle the weeds when we do downward dog."

Fable bit her lip, unsure if she was ready to leave the quiet safety of the stable. Nightwind rubbed his head against her arm as if urging her to go with her friends. He'd still be there this evening.

"Sure." She gave Nightwind's mane one last tug with the comb. "Just let me put these grooming supplies away first." She tossed the comb into the bucket she'd placed in the corner of the stall earlier. It was filled with an array of brushes, combs, elastic bands, and even a plastic spray-bottle labelled Mermaid Hair that Alice had concocted. Fable wasn't sure what was in it, but when she'd sprayed it on Nightwind's mane, the smell of fresh ocean spray combined with some sort of fruity flower had filled the stall. His silky locks had immediately curled into beachy waves.

She picked up the bucket and slipped from the stall. "See you later, Nightwind."

The pterippus curled his lips in a yawn.

Thorn backed up to give her friend room to enter

the aisle. "How are you feeling? Did the licorice root tea I made you help?

"If you noticed the extra zing, that was me," Brennus added. "It was my idea to add the ginger."

Fable's chest warmed at the care her friends had been giving her. Between tea, meditation sessions, herbal sachets, and not-very-good guitar music, her friends had been doing their best to help re-energize her.

"It was good." She smiled. "Very ginger-y."

Brennus's eyes creased with his grin.

Fable crossed the aisle to the tidy tack room across from Nightwind's stall. She hung the bucket on a hook above the leather harness the pterippus wore the day they'd left for Mistford. A day that seemed so long ago, before they knew anything about Orchid or the Order of the Jade Antlers. *Or the Blood Curse and its awful ingredients.*

She stepped back into the open barn area, her heart stinging at the thought of Star. She had wanted to go after her friend immediately, but Aunt Moira wouldn't hear of it. Fable had been too exhausted to argue—but fortunately, help had come in the form of new friends.

Fable looked at Thorn. "Have you heard from Orchid?"

The day before, despite Aunt Moira's objections,

Orchid and Sir Reinhard had set out to the Lichwood Forest, determined to save Star and her flock from Endora. Fedilmid had insisted they bring one of the speaking stones. Its partner now rested against Thorn's chest. Orchid had promised to be in touch every day with updates.

Thorn shook her head. "Only last night to let us know they made it to the ButterTub. They were staying the night there and heading into the Lichwood today."

"I hope they can release the firehawks," Brennus said.

Thorn nodded. "And every other soul trapped inside that mansion."

"Then burn it to the ground."

Fable had no idea what Orchid and Sir Reinhard might face once they got there. She was sure Endora was back inside her lair, nursing her wounds and plotting her next move.

Brennus gave her a sideways glance. "Speaking of burning—what is with those green flames you keep conjuring?"

Fable swallowed. She hadn't had a chance to speak with Fedilmid yet, but she had a hunch that this new magic had to do with her anger and fear. When they spun out of control, the flames appeared. Being a heart mage, her magic ran off her emotions. When she'd managed to think straight and reach for her light, no out-of-control fiery magic had surfaced.

"I need to talk to Fedilmid about that," she replied. "But I think I can learn to control them."

He nodded, his eyes shining with his usual mischief. "Good. I'd like to avoid being scorched every time I'm near you." He grabbed her hand and gave it a squeeze.

Fable squeezed him back, then glanced at Thorn. Another thought had been bothering her since they had finally found Orchid. "Do you think you're going to stay now that you've found your sister again? I know you don't feel comfortable in Mistford. And now that we're sticking around here for a while—"

"I'm not leaving." Thorn ran her braid through her fingers. "Not yet, anyways. I hope one day we can look for what's left of our colony. But Orchid's on this mission now with the Jade Antlers." She paused. "Besides, I'd miss you guys too much. Even you, Brennus."

Brennus snorted. "Admit it, you'd miss me most of all."

Thorn rolled her eyes. "I'll admit I'd miss you, but maybe less than I'd miss Fable. And Timothy." She raised her eyebrows. "And Grimm."

"You'd miss Grimm more than me?" Brennus gave her a mock look of sorrow.

Fable's heart lifted at her friends' banter. Subconsciously, she brushed her fingers against the pocket of her dress. The Blood Star lay inside it, hard against her thigh. A halo of warm magic surrounded it. There was no way her great-grandmother was going to rest now that Fable had the star. Stealing it back had been the easy part. Now, Fable had to protect it.

She followed her friends into the bright sunshine outside. They chatted amiably ahead of her as they wound their way to the back yard of the inn. Alice waved from her spot on the freshly mowed grass. Grimm, standing beside her, barked an excited greeting. Despite everything that had happened, her heart felt happy in that rare moment of normalcy. Nobody chased her. Her magic didn't writhe against her. The only bickering between her friends was playful banter. If only her life could always be like this.

Maybe it will be some day. Now that I have the magic of the star, anything is possible.

Right?

Epilogue

The chime above the door of the Drippity Cone jangled as Fable followed Thorn and Brennus into the sunshine outside. She wiped the napkin across her chin and took another bite of her sweet purple ice cream. *Blueberry cheesecake. Perfection.*

Beside her, Thorn took a big lick of her green avocado concoction. "It's too bad Timothy missed out on this again."

"I can't believe he'd rather hang out with Malcolm that come for the most amazing ice cream in all of Starfell." Brennus eyed the bright orange scoops on the waffle cone he held in his hand. "I'm glad you talked me into the apricot mango. It's even better than I thought."

"He'll get lots of ice cream this summer," Fable said. She spun on her heel to lead the way back towards the Thistle Plum. "Fedilmid's sure it's going to be hot and dry—"

She stopped in her tracks. A red brick building with

a slate roof and a crooked chimney sat beside the ice cream shop where the hardware store should be. A sign with a dragon wrapped around the words hung above the door.

Ralazar's Odd and Unusual.

"Brennus," Thorn said.

His hands dropped to his side and the ice cream slid from his cone to the sidewalk. He didn't seem to notice—or if he did, he didn't care.

Isla Tanager appeared in the glass door. Her long dark curls were swept back from her taut face. She cast an anxious glance behind her, then twisted the bolt of the lock and strode back towards the interior of the shop.

"Mom!" Brennus dropped the cone and sprinted to the door. He grasped the handle with both hands and pushed. The door didn't budge.

Fable and Thorn rushed to his side. Thorn squinted, peering through the window.

Brennus raised his fist to pound on the glass, but Thorn caught his wrist before he could knock.

"Ralazar's inside."

"What?" Brennus craned his neck to look up at her. He yanked his wrist from her grip.

Thorn jerked her head to the window. Fable peered through the dim light inside the shop and saw a man as tall as Thorn standing at the front counter. He wore long brown robes and his back was to them, but the red scales that covered his neck and bald head were clearly visible.

Brennus's parents both stood behind the counter with nervous expressions. There was a wire dog kennel on the countertop that held a mottled fluffy cat with pointy ears. Bart looked rattled, his face pale as he listened to the man before him. His boss. No, his captor.

"I can't hear what they're saying." Brennus frowned.

Thorn glanced at him. "Don't you know what's in the cage?"

Brennus shot her a look, but then pressed his face up against the glass of the door. His eyes widened. "That's a teakettler."

A teakettler! Fable had only heard that word in one other place—the Blood Curse recipe in her mother's journal. "Steam from a teakettler's cry." Her words were barely a whisper. "He's gathering ingredients for the curse. He's after the star."

"We don't know for sure," Thorn said. "Teakettlers are really rare. He could just be collecting rare creatures. Remember, Aldric mentioned him at the Magical Menagerie."

Fable peered back through the window. Bart opened

a drawer beneath the front desk. He pulled out a crisp white feather the length of Fable's arm and handed it to Ralazar.

Fable's heart lurched. "That's a pterippus feather. It looks just like Nightwind's."

Isla glanced away from the men and noticed the children at the door. Her mouth fell open and she shook her head, as if asking them to leave.

"We have to go. If Ralazar catches us here—" Thorn started.

"No," Brennus shot back. "He'll just think we're shopping. I need to talk to them."

The door of the shop began to rattle. Fable glanced up. The sign swung back and forth above their heads. She took a step back. "You guys . . ."

The storefront window shook and clattered. Something crashed within the shop. The whole store let out a groan.

"It's shifting!" Thorn grabbed the back of Brennus's jacket and dragged him away from the quaking shop.

He tried to twist away from her, reaching for the storefront.

Fable followed, her heart frozen against her ribs. "Come on, Brennus. We have to get away."

A tear streamed down his face. "No! What if they

don't come back?"

There was a loud rumble and a crash, as if the store had completely collapsed, but when Fable turned there was no heap of bricks or dust settling in the air. The grey stone wall of the hardware store sat where the Odd and Unusual shop had been seconds before.

People milled past them on the sidewalk as if nothing had happened. Nobody else seemed to have noticed the shift—or the fact that a completely different store stood beside the Drippity Cone.

Brennus wrenched his arm free from Thorn's grasp and shot her a look even sharper than one of Aunt Moira's warning glares. "Now what?"

Fable grasped his hand and gave it a squeeze. "Now we fix that guitar and find your parents."

Brennus stared at her with his tears in his eyes. "How?"

Thorn gave him a half-smile. "We always find a way."

"Because we're a team, remember?" Fable grabbed Brennus's hand and pulled him in to her side. "And we've got each other's backs. No matter what."

Follow Fable's adventures in Starfell Book Four:
The Curse of the Warlock.
Coming spring 2021!

Visit www.jessicarenwickauthor.com and sign up for
the mailing list to be kept up to date on future book
releases, events, and giveaways!

GLOSSARY

Algar Whimbrel (AL-gar WIM-bruhl) — a woodsman; Fedilmid's husband.

Arame (AIR-am) – a portal-caster; Endora's first assistant.

Brennus Tanager (bren-US) – Bart and Isla's son; Fable's best friend.

Burntwood Forest – forest on the east side of Starfell; previously the Greenwood Forest; where Fable landed when she first left Larkmoor.

Collector – a magical item enchanted to transport beings who set it off.

Endora Nuthatch (en-DOR-ah NUHT-hatch) – a lich; Morton's grandmother; Fable's great-grandmother.

Faari Nuthatch (FEH-ree NUHT-hatch) – Morton's wife; Fable's mother; deceased.

Fable Nuthatch (NUHT-hatch) – a sorcerer; Faari and Morton's daughter; Moira's niece; Timothy's cousin.

Fedilmid Coot (FEHD-ill-mid) – a witch; Algar's husband; also known as The Fey Witch.

firehawk – a wild chicken that breathes fire and reads auras; Star's species.

Folkvar (FOWK-var) – a giant race of people who live in colonies and off the land; Thorn's race.

Grimm – the Nuthatch's loyal mastiff.

Larkmoor – non-magical town separated from the rest of Starfell by the Windswept Mountains.

lich – a magic-caster who gains power by evil deeds; drawn to power to and immortality.

Lichwood – the forest on the west side of Starfell; where Tulip Manor resides.

Mistford – magical city in the south of Starfell.

Moira Nuthatch (MOY-ruh NUHT-hatch) – a witch; Thomas's wife; Timothy's mother; Fable's aunt.

Morton Nuthatch (NUHT-hatch) – Faari's husband; Fable's father; Endora's grandson; deceased.

Orchid (OR-kuhd) – a Folkvar; Thorn's sister.

Rose Cottage – Fable, Timothy and Moira's home in Larkmoor.

sorcerer – a person who's magic comes from within.

Star – a firehawk; Fable's first friend and guide in Starfell.

Stonebarrow – industrious city in the north of Starfell.

The Buttertub Tavern – a pub between the Burntwood Forest and the Lichwood; halfway between Mistford and Stonebarrow.

Timothy Nuthatch (NUHT-hatch) – Moira and Thomas's son; Fable's cousin.

Thomas Nuthatch (NUHT-hatch) – Timothy's father; Moira's husband; Morton's brother; deceased.

Thorn – a Folkvar; Fable's best friend; Orchid's sister.

Tulip Manor – Fedilmid and Algar's stone cottage in the Lichwood.

undead – corpses raised from their graves by a powerful magic-caster.

Windswept Mountains – mountain range that cuts across the west of Starfell.

witch – a person who draws magic from the earth.

wizard – a person who learns magic from books.

Acknowledgements

Here's another heartfelt thank you to all my friends and family who have encouraged me along the way with my Starfell books. All of the hours poured into this project, the late night writing and editing sessions, and weeks of meticulous planning wouldn't be possible without you. I am so grateful to have you all in my life.

A special thanks again to my wonderful editor, Talena Winters (without her, these books would not hold the magic that they do), my proofreader and childhood friend, Erin Dyrland, my partner and biggest cheerleader of all, Russ, and my close group of friends who have believed in me right from beginning!

Lastly, the overwhelming support I've received for this series has been a pleasant surprise and I am so grateful for readers like you. Thank you!

Jessica Renwick

About the Author

An avid reader and writer since she was a child, Jessica Renwick inspires with tales of adventures about friendship, courage, and being true to yourself. She is the author of the award-winning *Starfell* series for middle-grade children.

She enjoys a good cup of tea, gardening, her pets, consuming an entire novel in one sitting, and outdoor adventures. She resides in Alberta, Canada on a cozy urban homestead with her partner, fluffy monster dogs, four chickens, and an enchanted garden.

You can find her at www.jessicarenwickauthor.com , on Instagram and Facebook @jessicarenwickauthor, and on Goodreads. Independent authors rely on word-of-mouth. A review on Amazon, Goodreads, or your choice of bookseller would be greatly appreciated. Just a few words really do make a big difference.

Made in United States
Orlando, FL
27 May 2023

33522561R00200